TABITHA'S TRIALS

Tabitha is reluctantly released from St Mary's Establishment for Impoverished Girls because Miss Grimley will not break the rules and allow her to remain. She must go into service, contributing to the school so that other girls will benefit. Tabitha rides on the back of a wagon and watches her past drift into the distance. With a heavy heart, she contemplates years of hard work and predictability stretching before her, little realising just what the future has to offer . . .

1

Tabitha reluctantly climbed into the wagon behind the higgledy-piggledy arrangement of furniture. Although the array looked dishevelled it had been tied down firmly. She glanced at the tightly knotted ropes and thought miserably that she was amazed they hadn't done the same with her — to make sure that she didn't break free also. Folding her arms defiantly, she glared at the sombre figure standing before her. Dressed in a long, high necked, black gown was the severe figure of Miss Grimley, the person in charge of finding suitable positions for the young ladies educated at the establishment where Tabitha had been incarcerated for the past fourteen years. She looked up at the painted board at the side of the entrance gates and read the beautifully painted words, because she had written them herself, with pride, not of the place, but of her workmanship and skill — *St Mary's Establishment for Impoverished Girls*.

The grey stone building with its mock gothic towers had never looked welcoming to her before, but right now it appeared to offer her security, safety and sustenance. It was her home since she was left, near to death, on its steps all those years previously. Thrown outside of its high walls and sturdy iron gates, where would she find those things now? There would be no Miss Grimley to mock and make her friends laugh as Tabitha imitated the woman's severe gestures and sombre expressions. No one would be there to turn to when a situation presented itself, or even just to talk to.

'I don't want to go, Miss Grimley,' Tabitha declared, for what she presumed would be her final time. The words had been uttered repeatedly to the woman over the last few days. They seemed to hang in the still air between them. 'Tabitha,' Miss Grimley replied, 'I chose your name wisely. You came back from near death as if St Peter himself had granted you life again, like he did to your namesake in the Bible. You surprised us all. Now it is your time to repay us by earning your keep and giving some other poor child a chance in life, like you have been given.'

Tabitha's heart felt heavy. Over the years many of her friends had been 'found positions' in the world beyond those gates, never to be heard of again. Whatever had happened to them? Were they all happy or dismally resolved to their fates? Did anyone care so long as the place that groomed them thrived? She had counted the days with dread as her own birthday approached. This of course was based on the anniversary of the day she was found. She had been deemed ready to face the world. Tabitha had tried to become an essential part to the smooth running of the home. She stared imploringly at Miss Grimley; the woman did not give away any glimmer of emotion. In fact, the woman's mouth was set in its characteristically thin line. It was two days since Tabitha had turned one-and-twenty.

She hugged her shawl tightly to her slender body. 'I would be of more use to you here!' she added defiantly, her voice becoming more frantic as she realised that the driver of the wagon was about to take his seat ready to move the vehicle forwards. 'Please, Miss Grimley, can you not speak to the governors on my behalf? They might let you take me on as your own personal helper!'

Tabitha had never begged or pleaded for anything before. She had taken every hardship, caning and punishment with a set determination to survive and overcome the system that she was being forcibly moulded into obeying, but this was different; out here there were no walls, no known authority and a very uncertain future. For a moment Tabitha thought she saw a slight flicker of hope, a softening in the woman's eyes, but as the wagon's wheels slowly started to turn, Miss Grimley shook her head defiantly. 'Impossible, girl . . . no, forgive my error, for I should say, woman! We'd have every one of our girls wanting to stay here instead of facing their future and repaying the debt to the home. Instead of having girls we would become a home filled with old maids!' For a moment their eyes locked at the irony in her words as Miss Grimley's cheeks flushed, as she had described her own status. 'If you don't go and work, how do we sustain the place? No, Tabitha, don't be so selfish! Your happiness is not something that is a God-given right. Do your duty. Life is not to be merely enjoyed, wasted on idleness and immorality, Tabitha, but to be steadfastly endured! Be an obedient servant, or your own life will end in poverty and you will be no more than a worthless wretch. Honour your master, work diligently and remember to be humble . . . and a grateful servant! You have been given the chance to have a life outside these walls. Embrace it and do not abuse it.' Miss Grimley did not give her the chance to retort. She walked briskly inside the compound behind the highly ornate iron gates. They were closed with a great cacophony of metal grating against metal; the sound seemed to echo within Tabitha's head — they had been locked, but this time she was on the outside, and she felt it was a cold and lonely place.

The wagon bumped along as it was taken over the well-worn ruts. The furniture upon it was not hers. She was to be deposited, like so much 'chattel' at the toll gate on the road south where her 'master' would have her next transport sent to pick her up. She had no idea what that would be, but as her body jerked to the movement of this rustic vehicle she hoped it would be a good deal more comfortable.

The sky was overcast, and the day cool. She had no coat, only one old woollen shawl and a few coins to her name. Her only other possessions, a complete set of spare clothes, were in a cloth bag, which she gripped tightly in her hand. She held onto it looking to the sides of the road. If highwaymen, or women, tried to make off with her few things she'd fight them. Those few items represented her life.

Tabitha thought she would be far more comfortable if she were allowed to sit at the front. However, the driver did not stop and ask her to sit with him. She tried to turn to take a good look at him. His shoulders were broad and his back very straight, the poise of a gentleman, she thought, but his lack of concern for her made her think he did not have the manners of one. The large greatcoat and hat he wore all but blocked any visible sign of his hair or features. Almost as if he were reading her mind, he slumped and jerked the wagon into a quicker pace. It was as if he had sensed that she was watching him and had not taken kindly to it. So she held the side of the wagon as firmly as she could as it trundled and bumped along. It was inevitable that with such a precarious grip Tabitha would be shaken loose. She landed on the road with a bump. Tabitha was shaken and for a few moments she was disorientated. The wagon kept moving on. She shook out her skirts and picked up her bag with more than a hint of frustration and annoyance.

There was no alternative but to walk on behind it until she could catch up with him. The road had a treacherously uneven surface, dry and rutted, so she tried to place each step swiftly without falling or tripping over again, but despite her uneven gait it was good to walk a while as her rump had become somewhat numb with being jarred against the unyielding wood of the wagon. Only when she heard horses approaching from behind her did she quicken her step and tried desperately to climb back upon the vehicle.

'Driver!' she shouted still angry at his total lack of concern for her comfort and well being. 'Slow down, sir . . . I've fallen off!' She raised her voice as loud as she could over the noise of the wagon, but if he heard her plea he did not heed her words. 'Please!' she yelled. It slowed and Tabitha struggled to get a firm hand hold on something on the wagon in order to pull herself up onto the back of it once more. She found one and, with a final pull, she heaved herself up. It was with more than with a little shock that the small stool she had been gripping broke free from where it had been tethered. The wagon wheel dropped down another rut and the stool came loose in her hand and both she and it landed unceremoniously on the road.

Picking it up and cradling it carefully in her arms Tabitha knew from her sore ribs that it had landed upon her first, and therefore was not badly damaged, as she had taken the impact of the fall; just a small scratch to one of its legs. She could not manage to climb back up again, especially with a bag held in one hand and a stool in the other. Tabitha tucked the latter under her arm and resolved herself to the fact that she was in for a long walk. It was then that the riders arrived by her side.

She stood still. The militia man pulled his horse up next to her. Tabitha clung on nervously to the piece of furniture and her bag as she looked up at the red-jacketed figure.

'Give it up, girl!' the man's gruff voice ordered accusingly.

'Pardon?' she asked nervously. The man had stopped her in her tracks. His horse twitched nervously as he held the rein firmly. The animal's large eyes seemed to stare wildly at her. She could see the wagon was still moving further away from her. If anything, the driver was quickening its pace. 'Give what up, sir?' she asked bemused

She saw the man's eyes looking at the stool, and she smiled, realising what he was thinking. 'It fell off the wagon,' Tabitha explained, wondering what Miss Grimley would make of her being thought of as a thief, and so soon after leaving the home.

'Yes, I know it did!' His facial expression was more of a sneer than a friendly smile, most unbecoming and, Tabitha decided, intimidating. 'I saw it 'fall' and your hand helping it on its way.' He bent down and took the stool off her with a sharp tug. There was something menacing about his manner. He looked at his two men. 'Put this back on the wagon and tell the driver we have apprehended a thief stealing his wares. Then, Williamson, take her to the lock up. She can stay there until the local magistrate arrives next week.'

Tabitha could not believe that the man could get his facts so wrong. 'You are mistaken, sir. I am not a thief. If you ask the driver, he'll tell you he was only giving me a lift to the toll road — where I was to be collected.' Tabitha tried hard to explain her circumstances. Each word she uttered only made the situation sound worse; an unchaperoned female sitting on the back of a wagon being taken to a turnpike road to be collected by a man she had never met, but who would know her by her letter of introduction. She placed her hand in her pocket to produce it, but was instantly dismayed as it was empty. The letter must have fallen out when she fell. Fool, she thought, for she had been so busy pleading with Miss Grimley to stay that she had not paid it any attention, not even taking in the name upon it. She could not even say what or who the man was, just that Mrs Grimley knew of him and had vetted him as suitable. That was all there was for her to know.

He swung down with one swift gesture and grabbed the back of her dress behind the nape of her neck. 'Never! Never speak to me unless I order you to.' His grip tightened until she was almost standing on tiptoe. The side of his saddle hurt her as he pulled her in towards the horse. It smelled. Tabitha was scared the animal would stamp on her foot. 'But . . . I . . . '

Tabitha tried to tell him that he was wrong.

He responded by releasing his hold on her and throwing her to the ground like a rag doll.

The soldier returned from the wagon. Tabitha stood up; she was shaking as much with indignation as fear. Now the horrid man would see the error he had made and he would have to apologise to her. She stared defiantly at him, waiting for the younger soldier to speak. She would demand that he make his apology in front of his own soldiers.

The soldier, Williamson, was grinning — not at her, but at a small bottle that he was holding in his hand. 'I tried to explain to him, sir, but he's been swigging this.' He held out the bottle to the senior officer.

The man took it and sniffed it. His face contorted as if with disgust. 'French brandy.' He shook his head. 'Can he answer any questions in his present state?' the man snapped at the soldier.

Tabitha started to feel a cold apprehension churning in her stomach. If the driver was drunk, who would explain to him why she was there and what she was doing? Or rather, that she wasn't doing anything untoward.

'No, sir! The horse must know the way because he is just holding the reins and . . . humming.' The soldier chuckled.

'This is no laughing matter, Williamson! The country is going to the dogs, thieves abound. That is contraband. Impound the wagon, we'll search it and he can answer our questions once he has spent a night sleeping on the stone slabs of a cell in the gaol.' He stared back at Tabitha. She averted her eyes and swallowed. She had to try one last time to make him listen and see that she was not doing as he thought but, in fact, was trying to climb back up. Whoever the man was, he was in his own trouble, although she thought that he could not be as drunk as they presumed for he had been sitting so straight not long since and had not sung a note to her. But where did that leave her? She had been found in the presence of a drunken laggard swigging contraband. Her stomach tightened involuntarily. Was this what the world would be like outside the the grey wall of St Mary's?

'Sir, this is a travesty . . . Miss Grimley of Saint Mary's . . . ' She had stepped forward to try to appeal to the man against his misunderstanding and the injustice which had befallen her. Her words were cut short when she felt the back of his hand strike the side of her face. Tabitha was stunned. She stumbled two steps back holding her flushed cheek. How dare he treat her so! She tried to choke back the tears that instantly filled her eyes at the shock of the blow.

'Take her to the cells and tell Bramble she is to have no rations today. She can talk as much as she likes tomorrow, when she is ordered to!' He pulled his horse's reins so that the animal moved around nearly knocking Tabitha over with its rump.

Tabitha's remonstrations were soon stopped as she was bodily thrown across the soldier's horse and, as he rode apace to the nearest lock up in the market town of Darnley, she felt both nauseous and wretched. By the time she was pushed off the horse then almost dragged to the cell still clinging to her small bag, she was cold, disorientated and scared half to death. Where was Miss Grimley now? She just repeated over to herself the words, 'It's a mistake, that's all . . . a mistake,' and prayed that in the morning all would be put right, for it had to be, hadn't it?

2

Two rats ran past her as if they cared not that she was there — she wished she could feel the same level of apathy toward them. Tabitha had tried standing up straight to avoid sitting - or worse, lying down on the cold stone floor. It was wet in places and the few areas that were covered with any straw at all, were far from fresh. The place smelt dank; it made her shiver with an icy feeling of dread.

She saw the isolated bucket in the far corner and knew what it was for from the smell that permeated the air, but tried hard to go no nearer to it. Tabitha had not cried for a long time but this was enough to make her miserable almost beyond tears; the fear and isolation — except for the rats — threatened to overwhelm and consume her senses. She stood, numb, like a statue frozen in time, trapped in her moment of disbelief — the realisation of her situation made her shake, for it was well known that they hung thieves! Perhaps this was hell and she was already dead, but then hell was said to be a hot place full of burning flames, from what she had been told by Miss Grimley. Surely, she reasoned, a place as cold as this was not for a person to be kept in, particularly when she had done nothing wrong. Tabitha started to think about the wagon's driver; only he could explain the situation fully. If they wouldn't let her say who she was or where she was from, then she would be released when he spoke the truth to them. However, he'd been drinking French brandy. If they wanted to know where he'd bought it they'd not be lenient with him, or her. What would he care if she was innocent or not? He was going to have his own neck stretched if he was dealing in contraband. Tabitha stared at the bars high up in the stone wall. The grey light that filtered in did nothing to raise her spirit. 'Oh God,' she pleaded, 'help me, please?' With her eyes closed she was lost in the moment — a prayer borne of pure desperation, wondering if she gave in to her need to cry would it help her at all, or should she save her energy and fight the urge and her fear?

'Now, he might just be a little busy at the moment, lass, but I can help yer a little, if yer pays for it, deary.' The gruff voice surprised her, was loud and made Tabitha jump. She spun around to see a squat built woman standing in the open doorway, holding in her hand a large iron ring with keys threaded onto it. Tabitha wondered if she could be her much needed life-line, but an angel she definitely was not. Her hair was a greasy grey, held in a grubby old cloth bonnet; her face was craggy and hard.

'Who are you?' Tabitha asked nervously.

'Well now, lass, let's see. How shall I introduce myself? I'm your best friend or your worst nightmare. It depends on how yer look at life, I expect. See, I arrange for folk's creature comforts in here. I decide who eats what, who gets fresh water and who sleeps where . . . and . . . with whom.' She sighed. ''Tis a great burden for sure. If I get it wrong folk can go hungry, thirsty, or get all mixed up together.' She stroked Tabitha's cheek with a finger. 'So smooth, so young, and so pretty. You could make a quick penny if yer was to use that fresh skin of yours to give comfort to others.' She winked then and grinned at her and Tabitha shrank away from her touch. 'Ah, I see, you are still an innocent child! Enjoy it whilst you can, lass. Now then, if I was to get you mixed up with old Ned, for instance . . . ' She leaned over to her as if to whisper next to Tabitha's face who flinched and tried not to balk at the woman's foul breath. 'He has the pox — one of 'em, anyways; I'm not sure which one as I don't get close to him, no-one does if they 'as a choice, that is. If you were to be mixed up with him, well, that would be a real shame, that skin of yours would be ruined. Or if I was to mix you up with Fred Black,' the woman shook her head and her cloth bonnet flopped around her dirty hair, 'that would be fine for him, but a night you'd not forget in a hurry. No, all these decisions rest with me, but a person's life can be improved by the clink of a coin. I'm not heartless, lass. I could get you a blanket or two, even find a cot for you and a little privacy, but these things don't come cheap. Everythin' in life costs summut, so what have yer that yer can share with me, eh?'

'But I'm not well to do,' Tabitha replied, panic rising within her. She had no one who could pay this woman off.

'You don't need to be rich, lass,' she said, and stared hard at her.

'I've done nothing wrong, ma'am, this is all a mistake . . . a big mistake.' Tabitha saw the look of sarcasm come upon the woman's face. She didn't believe her, and even if she did, Tabitha guessed, she cared nothing for the truth of the matter.

'Oh, I know that. I understand. You see it's always a mistake, my lovely. Everyone in here, is here because they made a mistake . . . the same one, they all got caught!' She laughed, a huge guffaw that seemed to fill the stone-walled cell.

'If you could only get a message to Miss Grimley she could put things right. She'd pay you, honest she would.' Tabitha could see a spark of interest in the woman's eyes.

'Have money, does she?' The woman raised a quizzical eyebrow.

'Aye, she runs the Saint Mary's home for Impoverished Girls. It doesn't look grand from the outside, I know.' Tabitha saw the woman look down when she mentioned the building — it was not a rich private school, but decided if she bent the truth, this woman may unwittingly help her. 'But Miss Grimley is a bit like you, see, she makes the girls . . . comfortable.' This could be her chance, so she tried to lie convincingly.

Tabitha had her attention.

'My name is Bramble, Hester Bramble.' She grabbed Tabitha's bag from her hand. Rudely, she rifled through it and found the small pouch with her few coins deposited within. 'Ah, so this is yer lot, is it?'

'It's all I have with me, but if you go to Miss Grimley she'll see you right. Honest she will!' Tabitha did not have to act to look sincere; she hoped what had started as a lie, was actually true, for hadn't Miss Grimley always had a special respect for her?

The woman took the pouch and placed it in a pocket within her ample skirts. 'This'll get yer a blanket, a crust to eat and something to drink. I don't hold with starvin' folk, and we'll see about sending a lad over to your Miss Grimley in the mornin'.'

'The morning!' Tabitha exclaimed.

'Aye, can't have a young lad runnin' around the moors at night now, can we?' She shoved the bag back at Tabitha's chest. 'Now, you're a good girl, yer not goin' to give me any fuss, are yer?' Bramble pointed a stubby finger at her face.

Tabitha looked at the blackened nail. 'No, ma'am,' Tabitha said dully, irate that this woman should steal from her when she had no way of defending herself. The whole situation was both unfair and intolerable, yet she had to tolerate and survive it.

'Good, lass, you and me'll get along just fine. You'll not have anything to bother about this night then, and we'll see what tomorrow brings. Every day is a new one!' She waved back at her as she left, and Tabitha glared at the sight of her back, and shuddered as the door slammed shut. The heavy metal bolts were shoved into place, and an icy cold silence fell upon her world once more.

★ ★ ★

The soldiers had removed each piece of furniture from the wagon one at a time. They had uncovered bags of salt,

24

tobacco and even a bale of silk hidden within the innocent looking cargo. 'He'll not see daylight for some time.' One soldier looked at the drunken figure of the driver slumped on the stone-flagged floor.

'What about his young moll?' He grinned at his friend. 'Should we go and interrogate her instead?'

'Why not? Bramble said she had no money on her and seemed as fresh as a daisy. Besides, we might get a reward for finding the drop site, if she should squeal under investigation.' He chuckled. 'Mind, she'll squeal, no doubt, anyhow.'

Simon waited until he was alone in the cell. The last kick from the soldier's boot had hurt but he had stifled his feelings as he lay prone, still pretending to be drunk, as if oblivious to the pain.

The floor was cold and unyielding. It had broken his fall but fortunately no bones when he was thrown into the cell.

His thoughts wandered from his own

discomfort to the whereabouts of the young woman. Simon felt the knot of guilt forming in his stomach. She was an innocent and had no part in any of this. He had been responsible for her well-being until he had passed her on at the turnpike road. Now look where he had brought her — to gaol! God help her, he thought; if he didn't or couldn't she would need some protection against those brutes.

Picking his time carefully he rose to his feet and leaned against the closed door. He glanced down. The fools, he thought, for they had shut it but not bolted the door firmly. Such had been their eagerness to go to the girl, whilst they thought he was out cold.

He opened the door carefully and slowly just in time to see them enter a cell at the end of the corridor. That told him where she was and gave him another dilemma, for the courtyard lay in the opposite direction. He could run now — unseen and save his own skin, but he was a man of conscience and honour, so the idea was not to be borne. He left the door to his cell open wide and left the courtyard door ajar. Timing was to be everything if he was to succeed with his plan.

★　★　★

Tabitha heard the door of her cell being opened. She thought it must be the food and blanket that she had paid so dearly for.

Two soldiers stepped inside the room. Tabitha's heart leaped with joy for a moment as she thought the mistake must have been realised and she was to be released. She smiled at them and stepped forward, but they closed the door behind them, shutting it firmly with one hand. They smiled back at her, but their smiles held no warmth; instead they filled her with an ice cold dread. The realisation that they had not come to free her hit her hard; she was trapped in a room with two strange men.

3

'I'm innocent! I did nothing wrong. I didn't steal anything from the wagon. You must believe that!' Tabitha shouted, desperately trying to make them back away from her, but instead they were moving forward and cornering her. 'I'm not a common girl. Stay away from me!' Tabitha exclaimed, as the two soldiers looked from one to the other and then back at her.

'Well you're no lady, lass, and now is a good time to learn how to make your life a little easier. You need to 'cos highway robbery is a hangin' offence and you're real lucky because the assizes meets next week and Justice 'Freeman' ain't inclined like his name. He ain't for freein' folk. He's for stretchin' the necks of the vermin who rob from decent folk, ever since his good lady was robbed of her finery last

28

year.' He looked around the dank cell. 'However, I'm a compassionate man and so is me friend.' He grinned at her, and then looked down at the floor. 'Not very homely in 'ere is it? Not even a blanket.' He shook his head. 'Jethro, go and get the one from the driver's cell. He won't be needin' it, but we will.' He winked at Tabitha, placing a firm hand on her shoulder as she tried to slip past him as Jethro left the door tantalisingly opened behind him.

'What?' She saw the look on his face and was in no doubt. He was a vile creature. 'This is a mistake, I . . . don't do . . . '

'Yes, so you say, but tell me, do you think all girls are born either good or bad? No, lass, it's need and circumstance. Right now I have a need and you have a 'circumstance'.' He grinned at his own quip.

Tabitha now realised that she was left with one determined, heartless bully, and wondered if this was her chance to escape. However, that would not only make her a victim of injustice, but an outlaw — who'd believe she had run away from a soldier for her own safety. Who would care?

He shook her hard. 'I've tried to be nice to you.' He slammed her back against the cold, stone wall. He threw her shawl to the damp floor. Tabitha wriggled and tried to kick him in order to break free, but he was strong, big and used to fighting men. Tabitha knew she stood no chance of fending him off. She tried to call out for help. The woman, Bramble, would come to her rescue, Tabitha had paid her, but he stifled her cry with his mouth. Panic filled her; he was trying to touch her in the most personal places. She had never felt so threatened in her life.

'Seth!' The call from his friend could be heard from the corridor. He ran into the cell, his face looked shocked, ashen even.

'You'll have yer turn soon enough. Now place that blanket down here. I don't want to mess up me uniform.' He paused and stared at his friend. Tabitha was fighting back her tears.

'He's gone! The bloody driver . . . he's gone!' the soldier exclaimed. 'That bloody wretch, he's run off. He can't have been as drunk as we thought he was.'

Tabitha was instantly released. It was a cold gesture of being discarded. 'You bloody idiot, man! Did yer not bolt the damn door after yer?'

'No, but neither did you!' his friend answered. The two of them were completely absorbed in their own world. They ran to the men's cells, swearing and cursing at each other's stupidity.

Tabitha was up on her feet as soon as they were beyond the door. She grabbed her bag tightly for what it was worth. Slowly she peeped out of the doorway. A hand cupped her mouth gently. She was ready to scream but then she saw the dark features of the driver step forward from the shadows.

'Come with me,' he whispered softly.

'What have you got me into?' she replied angrily, yet her voice was barely audible.

'Woman, it's what I'm getting you out of that matters right now! Now, hush and come with me.' He ran down the passage to the courtyard door. She should have followed him without question, but she was so scared she hesitated a moment; realising her folly she stepped out of the cell and tip-toed along the narrow passage.

The doors to either side were bolted and locked. Without hesitating she ran to the end of the corridor that led to the courtyard. There were soldiers everywhere. The place was in turmoil. She couldn't cross the yard without being seen. Edging into the dark shadows Tabitha made her way towards the wagon; she froze as she heard the voice of the woman, Hester Bramble, becoming louder as they moved nearer to Tabitha.

'Have yer done with the girl, then, yer useless louts?' Her raucous voice shouted over the yard to the man named Seth.

Tabitha shrank down low into a squat position, hidden by the wagon wheel; she started to tremble.

'Hell no! But I paid yer well enough. We'll find him! You owe me, Bramble!' He wiped the back of his hand across his mouth. 'You best cover this mess up, Hester, or the skin won't stay on me back, and that's goin' to cost yer dear. Remember, woman, we go down and you will too.'

'Stop yer hollering' and start lookin' for him,' Bramble replied.

Tabitha was enraged. The woman had taken her few pence and the soldier's money also. She had never intended to help her at all. Tabitha could hear the woman shuffling nearer and her fear grew. Tabitha looked behind and then in front of her, but there was nowhere for her to run, the driver had gone without her — she was trapped. She heard a faint tapping sound from under the wagon. She looked underneath and was relieved as her eyes met his, as if locked in a moment of trance that could have brought the downfall of both, but instead, he urgently gestured to her with his head that she was to join him in his hiding place. The driver, sober as a judge — Tabitha realised the irony of her thought — was lying along a hidden ledge inside the wagon's false sides. He was showing her there was another such place along the opposite side to him. She quickly shuffled underneath the vehicle and rolled onto the ledge and lay there stock still. He looked alarmed as she stretched out, balancing precariously on the wood. Her eyes followed the train of his and she could see her skirt had fallen to the ground. Swiftly, she hauled it up and tucked the fabric firmly under her leg. Both lay motionless, staring at each other, both understanding that now was not the time to talk.

A scream was heard beside the wagon. 'You bloody imbeciles! Why do yer think we have bolts on the bloody doors — just to make 'em look pretty, eh? She's done a runner too!' Bramble's voice was bordering on hysterical.

'Where the hell can she have got to?' Jethro asked.

'I don't know,' Seth answered, 'But you best take that wagon and four men back to the turnpike road and get word out that we have two highway robbers on the loose. One man, late twenties, dark hair and tall, and one young woman, also dark haired, slight of build. Make sure they sound dangerous mind. Say the lass's looks are deceptive and that she is a harlot and he a villain. They'll not get far this night. Say there's a reward for information leading to their capture. I know where she's from so we'll soon have a name to put on the posters. Hurry, before his lordship returns and we're turned into cannon fodder!'

Tabitha stifled a sob, because she had spoken so honestly to the woman and now it was to be her downfall. She had repaid Miss Grimley and the home which had saved her miserable life by becoming a wanted highwaywoman, beyond the law and the pale. The man was staring at her. His expression upon his face showed what she thought was genuine concern for them both, she hoped. If she faltered now it was both of their lives at stake. She swallowed hard, controlled her fear and held on tightly.

The wagon moved off. It bumped and the dust and dirt flew up from the yard. Tabitha tried to cling for dear life to a rope that had been threaded through holes in the wood to provide hand holds.

The man opposite stared at Tabitha. 'Hold on tightly,' he mouthed at her.

It was advice she had not needed.

4

Between the dust rising from the road and Tabitha's inner fears, her mouth was becoming very dry making it increasingly difficult to swallow. She hung on tightly staring at the wood above her head, praying that the next jolt would not be her undoing. A vision of being hurled unceremoniously from the wagon, spread-eagled on the ground and crushed by the heavy wheels crossed her mind. She held on even tighter. Eventually, the vehicle slowed down and then changed direction as it moved off the road. Rough earthen track was replaced by cobbled stones. The dust abated, replaced by the noise of the horse's hooves striking against the hard surface. They had entered an inn's yard. As the wheels jarred on the uneven ground, the wagon was turned around. She dared herself to look across at the man opposite her. He could be a murderer for all she knew but then why would he help her if he was? He was staring back at her whilst both listened intently to the soldiers' animated conversation above them. There appeared to be an argument taking place.

'We were ordered to go to the toll road — not the inn!' a voice exclaimed loudly.

'Just the one, Seb, and then we'll be on our way — honest we will. No one will ever know and those two won't get far. What, a half-starved girl and a drunkard? Their bodies will be found out on the moor, I've no doubt about that so wet yer whistle. Come on, man. They cannot have overtaken us. Just the one, eh? If we look around the inn a bit — like in the back store room, we may even get a drink free dependin' on whose company they've been keepin' lately and where they've got their ale from. Contraband is big business round these parts.' He chuckled as if there was a hidden meaning within his words. Tabitha could not see the man wink conspiringly at his friend or she would have realised they too had taken their share of bribes.

'You'll get us both flogged one of these days, man,' the other said, as he gave in to the temptation of a jug of ale. Eagerly he walked inside the inn.

The wagon had moved slightly forwards as the men dismounted. Tabitha and the stranger waited till all was quiet before daring to move. She stared at the man. He seemed so very calm, almost as if this was an everyday occurrence for him. He smiled back at her, through a dust covered face, then winked at her before letting himself silently roll from the wooden ledge to the stony ground below him. Like a cat, he set himself crouched low on all fours and surveyed the yard. But he was not like any farm cat she had watched, Tabitha thought, more of a fine animal in its prime — a lion, strong, stealthy and astute.

He placed his hand on her arm gently. 'Roll off, miss, quietly and smoothly. Gather up your skirt. We leave our transport here,' he whispered.

Her head was filled with questions that she would like to ask him. However, the time for talking was not now. Tabitha did as he instructed her and was led, with her skirt bunched up in her hands enabling her to follow him, as they skulked around the back of the low thatched roof building. Necessity had put cares about modesty far from her mind.

'Are we to hide in the stables?' she asked nervously.

'He turned to face her and grinned. His teeth seemed unusually white against the dirt that covered his face. Deep brown eyes looked sympathetically at her from behind his dark lids. She found herself wondering what he would look like if he were clean, and dressed in decent clothes. A totally inappropriate thought for such a dire situation as hers, she dropped her skirt hem and cleared such thoughts from her mind.

'No, miss, for if they search they will look in all the obvious places of shelter — that being the most obvious one.' He led her by the hand behind the stables and into the trees that lined the inn.

'Where were you going?' she asked him, as she shook out her skirt properly, patting the dust off the fabric as best she could, aware that he had seen more of her legs than he should have. However, after the last few hours life and its rules of fairness and propriety seemed to have been shattered.

'About my business, miss. I was asked to collect you as a favour.' He looked at her seriously. 'You were not part of my original plan. You were supposed to be met at the turnpike. I'm so sorry you had to endure such an ordeal.'

Tabitha blushed and was at a loss for words. She was relieved when he continued speaking.

'So what to do now with you? They know who you are or soon will do. You therefore cannot go back from whence you came, nor forward to where you should be going. That gives us quite a dilemma.' He paused and looked at her as if deep in thought.

'You don't talk like a smuggler or an outlaw.' Tabitha saw a wide smile spread across his face. He shook his head and rubbed a hand through his dusty hair.

'I am relieved to hear it, but, tell me young lady, what would you know of either?' He stood and looked at her most earnestly.

'Nothing, I suppose. But I presumed they would speak like . . . like those soldiers — they are very common, coarse men.' She could not help but remember the disgust she felt at the soldier's aggressive behaviour toward her. Tabitha watched his features relax into a solemn expression.

'Well, miss, some do. I ask only that you don't judge me so harshly when you have no idea who I am. Now, we must cease this chatter and move on swiftly before we are discovered by those common and coarse men.' His eyes betrayed a glimmer of humour and perhaps, she wondered, sympathy at her plight.

'Move on to where, sir?' Tabitha asked cautiously.

'That is a very good question,' he replied, but did not offer any answer. Instead she followed him like a spaniel after its master whilst out on a shoot or a hunt. However, she was only too aware that they were the hunted. Was he a fox rather than a wild cat? Sly — hunted . . . she doubted it but he was an enigma. Tabitha fought the rising panic inside her; she was an outlaw and at that moment this total stranger was the only person in the world who she could turn to for help. Miss Grimley could do nothing for her, even if she knew what had happened and tried to; it would be too dangerous for her and could end in the ruination of the home. Tabitha's reputation lay in ruins. No respectable household would employ a girl who had spent time in the cells, and worse, run away with a man, who appeared to be a wanted 'smuggler'.

They walked in silence through a wooded gill and then up onto the open moor. She followed carefully in his footsteps, aware of the marshy land that lay all around them. Tabitha was ill dressed for such an adventure. The open spaces and the beauty of this wild and desperate land, however, was not lost upon her. He said nothing to her as they traversed the ground. She let him watch and listen for trouble, whilst Tabitha focussed all her energy on where she trod and controlling her inner fears. Slowly, a new emotion was replacing it as if filling up an empty hollow. She was, in a way, free of everything that had controlled her life before. The future she dreaded of working long hours in some dusty old mansion had faded as she saw the wild countryside around her. No cell walls or locked doors existed here — just a brutal natural beauty. At that moment she cared not where she was going so long as she was never held prisoner again in such a confined cold space at the mercy of such callous people.

A few hours passed by, and still they walked. Dark replaced light but still he did not stop until they had traversed a moor and crossed a dale in order to reach the shelter of an ancient forest. By this time, Tabitha's feet were sore, her body cold and her stomach empty. Her new found freedom was starting to falter in her expectations as her energy ebbed away.

At last he stopped and faced her. Without hesitation or asking her if she wanted him to, he placed an arm around her shoulders and pulled her close to him. 'You're cold and tired, miss. Here, let me warm you,' he said softly.

She could not stop herself from stiffening at his touch and he sensed her fear.

'Body heat is the only warmth we have out here. I do not mean you any harm but we need to survive. Trust me, then we shall find some food and shelter.'

She did not reply instantly and he sighed at her indecision. Tabitha pulled away from him, but he ignored her efforts and wrapped his arm around her firmly.

'You are cold, woman! I give you my word that I'm not going to take advantage of you,' he told her and pulled her to his side. He walked her swiftly into the dim light of the forest and up an overgrown path. There he stopped and looked at her thoughtfully.

'Where are we going?' Tabitha asked feeling the warmth of his body next to hers and, unashamedly, being glad of it. 'Who are you?'

'We're going . . . '

A figure emerged in front of them wearing a cloak and a scarf tied around his face so that only his eyes were visible between that and his hat. The pistol he held was pointed at her friend's chest. Tabitha gasped and tried to pull away to run into the depth of the forest but her friend tightened his grip as more shadowy figures emerged — dark figures, like ghosts in the night. It was then she realised that they were surrounded.

5

'What went wrong?' the figure holding the pistol asked her companion directly. He still held the weapon firmly trained on him. The stranger's tall frame, wrapped in the cloak, accentuated his stature.

'I followed your instructions to the word, including collecting the girl.' He glanced at her as if silently trying to reassure her. Then his focus returned to the stranger and his expression was sombre once more. 'The militia came. They rode along-side the wagon and started to nose around in the load. There was nothing I could do but feign drunkenness and pray my chance to escape came. I awaited my opportunity to make a move. However, it did not happen until we were in the gaol.' He held Tabitha firmly in his grip, giving her a little momentary squeeze, she thought, of comfort, although it had not worked. She had decided against moving further, not even the smallest muscle. 'As soon as they found the booty on the cart we were both arrested, myself and the girl here.'

The man lowered the pistol and placed it in his belt. 'You were lucky to get out of there. Tell me, how did you? Or tell me, did you two cut a deal with the soldiers?' He looked around them at the forest's silent shadows. The men that surrounded them held pistols. Tabitha also watched and listened to every sound.

'You know me better than that . . . ' the man next to her answered defiantly.

'Do I?' interrupted the other. Tabitha could not make out if he was serious or if there was a note of sarcasm in his tone. Although they obviously were acquainted, neither spoke their name to the other. Tabitha thought this very mysterious and disturbing.

'Yes! And what is more, you know damn well you can trust me with your own life!' The swift reply was spontaneous.

'But not, it appears, with my goods!' the man retorted. 'Once more you have cost me dearly. So, now you are officially an outlaw. Congratulations, so tell me what do you intend to achieve next in life?' the man asked sarcastically and approached them. His eyes were also a deep brown, and Tabitha stared into them as if mesmerized. He was confident, she could see that, his manner authorative, yet easy, and his clothes were so fine of quality. Could he be a common highwayman? She doubted it, as there seemed to be nothing common about him, but if not, what was he?

'I shall stay low for a while. Follow you to the hall then go to the hermitage and wait for the search to stop. No one will be any the wiser that I am there. If you need me, send word; if not, then send food and some of your best brandy.'

He seemed to relax and loosened his

grip slightly on her arm. Tabitha was glad as it made her feel more tense — as if she was now a hostage. What was to become of her? Was she to stay holed up in this 'hermitage' with a strange man? It was only a matter of hours, not days, since she had left the monotonous existence in the home. Yet, now, she had been thrown headlong into the world — a dark world of mystery and danger.

'And you? Will you say anything of this, miss?' the cloaked man asked her in a gentleman's voice, not threatening in manner — but what appeared to be an earnest one.

'No!' Her voice was louder than she had intended it to be, keen to stress her point. But in the silence the word had hung ominously in the air. 'Because I cannot tell people what I do not know. Besides, you forget, I am an outlaw also and I don't know any of you, do I? They did not believe me at the barracks when I told them the truth and I cannot see why that would change. I am now a runaway. Those men are . . . brutes.' She still stared at his eyes. They did not mock her as he watched and listened to Tabitha's words. 'I cannot return to the home to take refuge, for Miss Grimely would be appalled at what has happened to me so far and I . . . ' she searched for the right words, 'I am a victim of circumstances beyond my control.' She tried to sound confident despite her returning fear.

'Miss, you are from the home for Impoverished Girls. Therefore, you know nothing of the outside world and have fallen foul of it. We shall make sure you fall no further.' His manner was again most polite and not one she would associate with a ruffian.

'Yes, I am. Do you know the home? Are you an acquaintance of Miss Grimley? Can you help me . . . could you talk to the governors on my behalf? Perhaps they would listen to you, sir.' Tabitha had felt hopeful for a moment but her question brought a ripple of laughs and guffaws from one or two of the men as she spoke. She had much to learn of this strange world and felt ill equipped to deal with such a situation.

He averted his gaze, staring at her companion. 'I hardly think they would listen to me, either. However, you will be found a place of safety to stay. What is your name?' he asked her. The man she had travelled with released his hold completely.

'Tabitha Quick,' she replied. 'And you are?'

'Well,' he smiled then repeated, 'Very well. From henceforth you shall be known as Dorcas Sprite. We will find you somewhere safe to rest and you shall forget all that you have seen here, but when the time is right you will be moved away from these parts. Do not speak of us . . . or you shall not speak again.' He fixed his stare upon her then bowed to her as she watched him wide-eyed. How sweetly he could threaten her life, and yet, she did not doubt that he meant what he said.

As he straightened up she could

smell a perfume, or was it a mixture of herbs? The fresh waft was fleeting, but it was a strange reminder of something long since forgotten from her childhood. So distant a memory that she could barely recall it. Yet her senses had, and locked away in her mind there was a deep seated memory stirring within her.

'Dorcas,' she repeated and nodded, not at all sure it was a name she cared for. The light had faded and a cold mist was settling. The men led them to a clearing where horses with sackcloth tied over their hooves were being held.

'We shall disperse here. You go to the hermitage. I shall leave the girl at the hall. She can work there for her keep. Agnes will see to her needs and make sure she is all right and the master of the house will be none the wiser.' The man paused as he looked at her thoughtfully for a moment, gave his instruction and was obeyed as men started to disappear into the night.

Dorcas was lifted bodily onto a

horse. The man with the cloak was going to climb up behind her. He held her horse's reins with one hand firmly. It was her stranger . . . her friend, her partner in this strange set of events who stood forward and swiftly mounted the horse behind her, placing a protective arm around her waist.

The man in the cloak released the reins and grabbed those of another animal.

'Very well. But you leave her at the hall, man, and travel on alone. You have inconvenienced the young lady quite enough. It is vital that you two are not seen together again.' He mounted the other animal. 'Well at least for now.' He paused for a moment as if considering something as he looked at them, then led the way through the woods.

As the horse twitched and moved nervously underneath them she was glad of the feeling of security that his strong arm gave to her.

'Sir,' she said quietly to her companion who had shared her precarious journey, 'I do not know your name. Therefore, I do not know to whom I am indebted.' She tried to sound relaxed, but she was feeling quite scared.

He looked at her and smiled. 'No, Miss Dorcas, you don't, and neither should you; for if we know names we can repeat them to the authorities. As for your debt, please just live long and be happy and you shall repay it in full.' He smiled at her through his dust-covered face and kicked the horse onwards, into the night.

'Where are we going, sir?' she asked, but to no avail. He did not say one word to her and left the forest by a different track. Their journey lasted for several hours travelling through the dark, with the occasional hoot of an owl breaking the silence. Tabitha, now Dorcas, was taken away from the impending danger of the cell and the soldiers, into a mysterious and strange future.

Eventually they rode up to the gates of an old mansion house. It was difficult to see the building properly as the light had gone and the clouds smothered the moon's rays. He jumped down to the cold earth and steadied the animal before she was lifted down from the horse, her rump sore from the long ride. Dorcas took a step towards a large door set back in the stone wall. Her friend remained as the other rider approached.

'Strike the door twice using the iron knocker. Say the word 'sanctuary' and enter. No questions will be asked and therefore no answers will need to be given.' He did not wait for her to raise her hand to the lion's mouth from which the knocker hung. The riders rode around the corner of the building and out of sight before the iron had struck once. Within minutes a figure dressed in a white nightgown and wrapped in a blanket opened the old door. A lamp was pushed towards her face.

'S . . . sanctuary,' 'Dorcas' said quickly.

The figure stepped out; a stocky woman wearing a clean cloth nightcap unlike the woman, Hester Bramble's. This lady was immaculately clean, her clothes having been well laundered and starched. She swung the lamp left and right then looked at Dorcas. She was covered in dust and knew she smelt far from fresh after her long and troubled journeying.

'Come in, girl, before you catch your death.' The voice had a warmth to it that made 'Dorcas' feel instantly at ease. She followed the plump figure into the kitchens. A fire still burned in the old hearth and a chair was pulled near it for her to sit on. The woman placed the oil lamp down and fetched over a tub, which was placed in front of the fire also. Without a word to her, the woman poured the water that had been heated on the fire's range into the tub, mixing it with cold water from an inside well. When she determined it was warm enough, she looked at a very tired and dirty, newly renamed, Dorcas and said simply, 'We'll be burning those dusty rags. From now on you wear our clothes and live here. Now you strip them dirties off and wash off that muck, lass. What's yer name?'

Tabitha looked at her, wondering if this was possible, that she could cast off her whole life with one tub of warm water — no matter how inviting. It was as if she was going through some ritual; ridding herself of her old life and starting anew, refreshed and clean.

'Dorcas,' she replied.

'Then remember it and that you have no other, not anymore. You strip and I'll fetch your new clothes. When you're clean, fed and rested I shall take you through your duties.' She looked at her then added, 'Well tomorrow will be soon enough.' The woman turned as if to walk away, then paused and glanced back at her. 'Tell me, lass, honestly — just one thing. Are you with child?'

Dorcas looked at her amazed at such a question. 'Absolutely not!' she answered, insulted at the woman's suggestion.

The woman chuckled. 'Good, then you're not one of his mistakes!' She shook her head, chuckled and walked off.

Dorcas slipped into the water and felt the warmth of the liquid on her skin. The woman knew who 'he' was, but who was the stranger in the hermitage? And where was it? She had no idea why she should care but she couldn't help her feelings and they told her she wanted to meet him again. The question gnawed at her, who was he?

6

Dorcas awoke late the next day. She had been allowed to sleep on a cot bed in a small room behind the kitchen. It was cosy despite the stone walls and floor. She only stirred when the bustle of bodies and cacophony of pots and pans became so loud from the kitchen that she was shaken from her slumber by then. Warmth permeated the room from the large fire in the kitchen next door. She could not help but hope that this was to be her own place here. It had all the aromas from the kitchen from the huge hearth and the bread making oven, which made her realise how hungry she was.

Looking around her Dorcas found a blue dress hanging from a hook on the wall, along with a white starched apron and bonnet. A pair of boots stood on the ground beneath them. Folded on the end of her cot were her under garments including long grey woollen stockings that had never been darned before. She felt the fabric's weave; it was much smoother than the coarse woollen cloth the home had used for their uniform. Underneath the folded garments was a simple brush and some hair pins. Dorcas wasted no time in changing out of the rather brief shift she had slept in, and then swept up her dark brown locks. She had silky hair the colour of rich mahogany that had a gentle wave to it falling just over her shoulder.

Once dressed, she took a deep breath and opened the door to her new world, boldly trying to face her future with strength and not without believing that this way, after all, was what the home had planned for her — a life in service. No one looked her way or paid her any attention as she nervously emerged from her small room. The kitchen was one blur of activity. Preparations for a meal were well under way. For a moment or two she watched the team work together for that was how they appeared. Could she be a part of it? Would they accept her and ask no questions? Again the doubts crept back in.

'Ah, there you are, Dorcas. Now, child, you shall start by taking this to the dairy across the yard.' The woman who had greeted her the night before placed a large jug in her hand. 'Fill it with cream. Ask Annabelle what you need to do and where things are, she'll show you. Ask her for a glass of milk for yourself as you've not eaten since arriving and have this as you go.' A piece of bread was placed in her hand. It was still warm, smelling tantalisingly fresh. 'Now be quick about it, we've guests arriving today, important ones, another Major and his wife, plus all the local squires.' She patted Dorcas' shoulder and almost pushed her out of the door into the yard at the same time.

Dorcas turned around and faced the kindly woman. 'Excuse me, but am I allowed to know your name?' she asked quietly.

'Haha!' The woman's rosy cheeks flushed. 'Bless you; you're as green as the cabbages. Of course you should know me name. I'm known as Sally or Mrs Bramble.'

Dorcas's smile dropped as she heard the woman's surname. 'Bramble!' she repeated, the fear and shock audible in her voice as she spoke it aloud with more than a hint of distaste showing in her face.

The woman looked at her, with a resolved expression, devoid of either humour or malice.

'Yes, Dorcas, I am Sally Bramble. It is a name that I am proud of no matter how others may have abused it. Now be about your business or I'll have you scrubbing the laundry floor instead!' Her voice sharpened and Dorcas backed away before turning around and running across the cobbled stones to what she discovered was not the dairy but a tack room. From the brief conversation, Dorcas decided that this Bramble knew, at least, that she had been in the gaol long enough to have met her namesake, Hester. Could it be possible that two women connected by name could be so apparently different? Perhaps, she reasoned, it was just an unholy coincidence but then why would she say such a thing about the name's abuse?

Her thoughts were interrupted as she entered the long room across the yard. She had never seen so many shiny pieces of metal and chains or polished leather. The care of them was immaculate. Whoever owned the hall was obviously proud of his horses and seemed to have only the best tack available for them. Dorcas started to eat the lovely fresh bread and pondered the skill of the pieces around her as she digested her food. She didn't mean to linger for long, or snoop around, but her curiosity had the better of her. She ventured to the little work room at the back, her attention taken by a large shiny brass buckle. It was an area divided from the main room by what looked like the side of a stable stall. She peeped around it and was surprised to see a man sitting on an upturned barrel polishing a well made pair of black boots. He had hair as dark as her own. She was going to tiptoe silently out, when the clatter of the metal jug she held in her hand hitting the wooden stall caused the man to look around.

'I'm sorry, I . . . ' Dorcas stopped mid speech as she stared at the deep brown eyes that were looking up at her. There was no mistaking him — it was her masked rider. He was tall and well dressed — in a uniform. He stood, reached up and removed the red jacket that had been hung on a hook behind him. How could the man in the woods be a soldier?

'I'm sorry to have frightened you, Dorcas. I merely needed some boot blacking before I presented myself to the guest.' He paused for a moment and then walked past her towards the open doorway. 'It is not something I would normally do for myself. However, as I was passing . . . ' he smiled at her. 'Soldiers' habits are hard to break. Were you hoping to fill that in here?' He looked at her and pointed to the jug.

'No, sir, not here but in the dairy, but I . . . ' Dorcas was pulling her senses together. She must have been mistaken, for this man could not be the cloaked man and be a soldier — that would make no sense. 'I'm sorry, sir. I entered the wrong building. She paused momentarily next to him as she was aware of that same sweet odour; she recognised it straight away. It was he, but she decided to act as if she had no idea, remembering his words — no questions. 'I can announce you, if you wish, sir.' She forced a gentle smile at him.

'Thank you, but I must not detain you from your chores. The dairy is next door, I believe.' He looked at her, the corner of his mouth curling up into what she could only determine to be a grin. 'I found it earlier . . . it looks rather like the tack room until you glance inside, that is. Good day, miss.' He walked off towards the front of the building.

She stopped outside and watched him walk confidently away. She couldn't help wondering if the hermitage was somewhere near. How could she find out without asking? That she could never do.

'I wouldn't go gettin' ideas on that one, girl. He's beyond your reach.'

Dorcas looked around to see a tall fine featured woman leaning against the doorway of the dairy. She was dressed in the same uniform as herself.

'Are you Annabelle?' Dorcas asked.

'Aye, that's me given name. Is that for me or were you sent here just to make eyes at the master?' She pointed to the jug.

'The master?' Dorcas questioned, repeating the words in a surprised voice.

'Aye, lass,' she laughed. 'That's the

Major; you're in his service, girl. They say he's as cool as ice. But I think he's . . . ' She looked dreamily across the yard.

'Are you two waitin' for the cream to turn to butter on its own account, eh? Or for the cows to go milk themselves perhaps?' The shout from across the square made them both jump gainfully.

'No, Mrs Bramble, the lass got lost that's all.' Annabelle was quick with her answer.

'Then now she's found, the pair of you do some bleedin' work!' the woman retorted angrily.

'Yes, ma'am!' They both headed into the dairy. Dorcas' mind was still confused. What was he doing the previous night? Who were those people and where was her friend in the hermitage? Were they all soldiers on some sort of clandestine mission? But that didn't make sense to her; it was not what she had been brought up to think of as even possible. However, her view of soldiers had changed rapidly of late.

69

If she could speak to him perhaps he would explain, but then as she entered the cool dairy rooms she felt a chill run down her spine, remembering the Major's words — ask no questions. He'd threatened her. But there was so much she wanted to know and needed to understand.

7

The first few weeks seemed to be lost in a strict routine of waking up early, setting the fires and preparing food. She was kept busy and always in or around the kitchen. No one asked from where she had come. However, equally everyone accepted she was part of the household staff now. Dorcas had learned to keep herself to herself and gradually her nervousness and apprehension left her. She wondered what secrets Annabelle and the others hid. There was no sign of a search for her and, although she often thought about the man who had escaped with her, she heard no gossip of him. If he had not come back to her she would never have been able to escape. She never ventured out into the upstairs part of the house and therefore had no contact with the Major. The food was good, though, and her little room next to the kitchen was her own space, of which she had become very fond.

'Dorcas,' the voice of Mrs Bramble called from the laundry room.

'Straighten your bonnet, girl. Take these shirts up to the Major's bed chamber. It's the large door at the end of the first landing. Hurry now, and don't you put a crease back in them after I've made them real fine for him.' The garments were carefully held out to her.

Dorcas thought to question her, as she had never been allowed beyond the servants' hall, but she was curious about the building which was now her home. She was very careful of her load and moved swiftly up the servants' stairs and onto the first landing. There the passage was covered in a rich carpet laid straight along the polished wood floor. Portraits of the previous owners stared down at her; she slowly walked along the corridor taking in all before her, wondering how much money a person needed to have to be like that. The house seemed so warm and colourful, unlike the stone walls and floor of her old home. Guilt occasionally gripped her as she remembered Miss Grimley telling her how she was supposed to be contributing to its keep. Instead, she was a discredited woman, living in hiding in this strange, yet comfortable new existence.

She opened the large door and walked boldly in, stopping abruptly in her tracks. Standing by the long rectangular window, staring out at the land he owned was the Major, wearing a long nightshirt. The light silhouetted his muscular form.

'Do you not normally knock, Dorcas?' he asked her casually.

'No, sir. That is, I don't normally come up here. Sorry,' she said, and immediately turned leaving the room and closing the door firmly behind her. It was then she realised that she was still carrying his shirts. She had no choice. Dorcas breathed in deeply, held her head high and knocked on the door.

'Enter,' the voice from inside commanded.

Slowly, she opened the door; he was still standing in the same place. He casually picked up the robe that had been laid across the bed, and covered himself for decency's sake. He had pride bordering on arrogance, Dorcas thought to herself, but tried not to show her opinion of him. Despite herself, she blushed.

'Your shirts, sir,' she stated the obvious and he smiled at her.

'Much better.' He pointed to a small room next to his four-poster bed. 'Hang them in there.'

She entered what was a narrow room full of outfits. All fine, and it seemed he had them specially made for every occasion. Dorcas hung the shirts quickly as she had been instructed and then noticed the riding boots and the distinctive crop. Above them was a fine, dark, riding coat. It was the scarf that caught her attention as she tripped on the corner of a hat box. It cascaded down from the pocket of a greatcoat that she fell into. It was black in colour and she recognised it as the one he had wrapped around his face the night she had been brought to the hall.

She tucked it back into the pocket and spun around to leave as quickly as she could.

The Major had followed her in and was standing watching her from the doorway. He was staring straight at her.

'I could accuse you of stealing, Dorcas, as now I find you with your hand in my pocket.' His face was serious and his voice cold.

'But I was putting it back . . . sir,' Dorcas answered in little more than a whisper and looked at him appalled at his suggestion. She could not help but be struck with fear as once again she had been witnessed replacing something to its rightful place, yet her honest act could be so easily misconstrued if he chose to accuse her of it.

She stared at him, at first guiltily, but

then she sensed he was toying with her in some way. 'Sir, please let me pass.' Her voice and manner had changed from whisper to one of forced confidence.

'Don't you like what you've seen, Dorcas?' He took a step toward her, blocking her way. He was barely a foot in front of her.

She swallowed but met the gaze from those deep brown eyes evenly. How different they appeared to be from those of the wagon's driver. His showed care, genuine kindness. 'It is not for me to say, sir. Please, let me pass so that I may complete my chores.' She was becoming annoyed with him as his face betrayed his enjoyment of her unease. Without hesitation he cupped her head in his hand and brought her lips to his. He kissed her, tenderly but firmly.

She pushed him away instantly and without hesitation slapped his cheek with the flat of her right hand. 'How dare you!' she exclaimed. Her nervousness had left her and anger had taken its place.

He laughed openly at her, stroking her cheek. 'Woman, I could have you at my mercy for daring to raise a hand to me. Do you not want a more interesting life than one spent down there with pots and pans for company? I can make your future easy. Think what it would be like to sleep in a warm bed each night: fine linen, sumptuous pillows. All you would have to do is occasionally share it with me. I would treat you to fine things such as good food. Your hands would be saved from many hours of scrubbing and blacking the kitchen's ovens. So, what do you say — the life of a servant or that of my mistress, indulged and pampered?' His question seemed to be made in earnest and she could tell he had been genuinely surprised at her action.

'Whatever you are, sir, you are no gentleman!' Dorcas snapped out the words. 'I have no ambitions to become your whore!' She was starting to panic. The feeling of being trapped in a narrow room brought back the memories of her disgust of the soldier's touch in the cell.

He placed a hand on her shoulder and laughed. 'Truce, Tabitha. No don't look surprised. I know, as you know, it was I who renamed you. So you may be an honest fool but you are no social climbing minx, good. Now, listen to me,' he pulled the door to behind them, 'Don't panic, woman, I needed to know your moral fibre. I am not in the habit of keeping opportunists or whores in my home. I also need to be able to trust certain people. Mrs Bramble informs me you have not gossiped nor snooped. So, if you will forgive my direct approach, I now believe you are of good enough character, and I have need of a 'good' woman, my dear.'

'To do what, pray?' she asked, not appreciating being put through more tests than she had already endured.

'To help out a mutual friend,' he replied simply. 'Now, return to your chores and I shall dress. Meet me in the tack room in one hour. Mrs Bramble will provide you with suitable clothes.

Go, for time is of the essence.'

'Is Miss Grimley in trouble?' Tabitha asked, thinking who else he could mean. But his blank expression when he asked, 'Who?' told her he must mean the stranger.

Without explanation she was dismissed and no apology was made. As if all had been carefully arranged before hand, she found a set of travel clothes laid on her bed. Without word or reason she dressed and waited for the rest of the hour to pass by and the next stage of her journey to begin.

8

Dressed in a long travel coat with a matching bonnet, Tabitha felt quite the lady. The clothes she wore were of a far better quality than a servant would normally have; certainly beyond her expectations. However, no instruction had been given to her as to where she was going, or why, which only served to add to the growing apprehension she was feeling. She had begun to like life at the hall. Having a room to herself, even a small sparsely furnished one, was more than she had been used to in the home. It had been warm too, with the smell of freshly cooked food hanging in the air.

'Ah, you look fine, lass,' Mrs Bramble greeted her with some mild enthusiasm. 'Now here is your bag. It has all the things in it that you might need for your journey. I hope all goes well with you and that you make a good life for yourself. You know all things work out in the future, eventually. It will be different, lass, and challenging, but think of it as a great opportunity for a lass, such as you.' The woman gave her an uncustomary hug.

'Where am I going, Mrs Bramble? Why do I have to leave here? I have a home here now, don't I?' She glanced around at the little room she had come to love as her own space. Then her eyes settled on the leather bag that had been placed by her feet. It was big enough to hold many outfits, but surely, she thought, this cannot be for her. She remembered the last departure she had made, on the back of a wagon, clutching her simple cloth bag with her one dress and few coins within it. There had been precious little else, certainly nothing that would need such a bag as the one before her. This was so strange and what did she mean, 'a lass such as her'?

'You want to stay here!' Mrs Bramble

repeated as if the thought amazed her. 'Mercy, Dorcas Sprite! You couldn't expect to be staying around these parts for long. You could be seen and then what would happen to us all then, harbouring outlaws. The Major's a soldier of rank and any of the regular men could be sent to him with a message. Anyone of them could recognise you if they'd been at the barracks when you were taken there. Think, lass, of the position he would be in if they turned out to be the ones who saw you.' She shook her head at the thought of it, her cloth bonnet flicking one way and then the other with her animated comments. 'Who knows what would happen. The Major couldn't help you if that happened — now could he? Think of more than just yourself here. The scandal would stick to him for helping wanted outlaws,' she shook a finger at Tabitha, 'Aye, it's no good flinching lass, because that is what you are in the eyes of the world. No, the furore it would cause could destroy his reputation. He'd be made a laughing stock!' Although the woman kept her voice low it lost none of its directness.

'You know . . . everything about me. How so?' Tabitha stared at the woman. 'Why did he help me and who was the man that aided my escape out of that horrid place?'

'You were told not to ask questions. Just be glad that he did help and hide you. You've been given a life, lass — grab it. Unlike me, and consider I am cursed with a sister-in-law that I would rather have nought to do with. Now enough of this gossip! Don't keep the master waiting. Get yourself gone and don't forget your bag, you'll need it, and lass . . . ' she placed a hand on Tabitha's sleeve, 'Don't cross him. He . . . well, just don't. What he's doing is for the best in the long run so you make every opportunity of it.' She winked at her and smiled then pointed to the bag.

Tabitha picked it up. Mrs Bramble's words had not given her any comfort whatsoever. There was a warning hidden within them as well as a promise of a better, yet uncertain future. The bag was much heavier than she had expected. She wanted to ask more; she wanted to demand answers and state her rights, but she realised there were no rights that she could claim — she had none. She was lucky not to be in front of the assizes, or back at the mercy of Hester Bramble and those brutes in the gaol.

Tabitha made her way to the door. 'Will I see you again, Mrs Bramble?' she asked quietly.

'No, lass, you won't.' The woman forced a smile.

'Then I shall say goodbye . . . and thank you for the kindness you have shown to me.' Tabitha left without looking back at her and walked anxiously into the tack room. She was met by the master of the house himself, looking every inch the Major as he was dressed in his brightly coloured uniform, not like the man with the scarf who had held a pistol trained at them in the forest. How different he looked; different, too, to how she had seen him an hour earlier.

'Good, you are present and correct. The carriage will be brought into the yard soon. You will travel in it to an inn. There, I shall meet you with a friend and you will be ready to move on to your destination. The pair of you will then travel on to the coast where your ship will be waiting. Once on board, all shall be explained to you in detail. You must . . . '

'Wait a minute, please.' Tabitha placed the bag on the floor next to her. 'What friend is this? What ship do you intend to 'ask' me to board? And where do you think I am going?' She held her arms in front of her nervously, as if trying to hold onto herself to give a feeling of security. She watched his cheeks flush with colour. He was a man used to making plans, giving orders and being obeyed.

'You are going to carry out my instructions, Tabitha.'

From deep within her a note of defiance rose up. 'Don't you mean — Dorcas? It was you who renamed me and took control of 'my' life; changing first my identity and now my future!'

'I repeat, you are going to obey my instructions. You shall now use your real name. I am telling you what will happen and you will obey simply because you have no other choice. You changed your own life when you stepped foot outside that ruin you referred to as your home.' He folded his arms. 'Beyond that fact, you should be exceedingly grateful to me as I have proved myself to be a friend to you. Here, your future is in ruins and I am giving you a chance to start anew, so stop being so selfish and think about someone beyond your own miserable existence. The gaols are filled with wenches who would gladly exchange places with you.' He kept his voice even, not raising it as if to be intimidating, but the simplicity and honesty of what he was saying to

86

Tabitha seemed brutal.

'You are talking to me as if you own my future and my destiny. Do I have any right to at least be consulted in your grand plan, sir?' Tabitha unfolded her arms but the fists that were formed as her arms hung by her side betrayed the frustration that she felt.

'No!' He sighed heavily. 'If you had arrived here as planned, Tabitha, you would have spent your best years working in my kitchens, but fate intercepted your arrival, so I am now offering you an alternative — a life to live for yourself with obedience only to one other.'

Tabitha was shocked. 'It was you who was to meet me at the turnpike?'

'Yes, I thought Miss Grimley would have given you the details. My brother was to bring you, with . . . well, with some goods that he was delivering to me. However, an unexpected arrival of the neighbouring militia intervened. Do not worry, your fee has been paid to the home. They will not lose out from this mess.' He walked over to her.

'It is as if you think you have purchased me!' Tabitha exclaimed, appalled at the brevity of her words.

'You could look at it that way, but I prefer to see it as more like a dowry has been paid for a young homeless girl — apologies, woman.' He smiled at her and picked up the bag.

'You intend to marry me?' she asked in disbelief; her feet seemed to be frozen to the spot.

He openly laughed at her. 'You are divine! I would accuse you of having high ideals way above your social station, but I think it is sheer naivety on your account mixed with ignorance — a beguiling mix of characteristics, even if totally misplaced. No, I have no intention of marrying you. However, I have a younger brother who you have already met, who has an amazing knack, like your good self, of landing himself in all manner of jeopardy. I am offering you both a chance to start life afresh. In order to settle his adventurous streak I

am set to match you two together. So . . . '
They heard the coach arrive outside.

'What if we do not wish to marry each other?' she asked defiantly . . . hopefully.

'That will not be the case for either of you. As I have already said, Miss Tabitha Quick, you have little choice in the matter, as the alternative is far from conducive to a happy life for either one of you.'

Tabitha swallowed as he walked away with her bag toward the doorway. 'You said the goods were yours . . . but they were contraband. That makes you a . . . '

'Silence your mouth woman! Or your journey will end here and now. Try telling them at the barracks what you have discovered and let's see whom they believe, shall we?'

'You mentioned a ship, sir. Where is it bound for?' She stared at the bag, knowing he was right; she had no one to whom she could go, and she doubted he would give her the chance. She looked up at him, defeated.

He stopped and glanced back at her, almost grinning. 'Wales,' he answered simply, 'South Wales.'

Tabitha was helped into the carriage and her bag lifted atop. He closed the door and gestured for her to lower the window so that he could speak to her.

'I trust you will find this comfortable enough. There is a small hamper tucked under the seat should you require refreshments. The journey will take approximately three hours. Think clearly along the way, young lady. You have been given a hand up in life to a better future, one that will see you attached to a family of position and fortune — mine! Do nothing to discredit them . . . or yourself.'

He waved the driver to go forward and the carriage wheels turned. Tabitha watched as her life moved on again. Marriage, she repeated the world to herself in her mind. She had never dared to contemplate it; beyond a possible match to a fellow servant at best, what chance would she have to marry as a kitchen maid? It just had not been seen as an option.

She tried to focus on the man who had shared such a ridiculously dangerous meeting as being slung under a wagon, with her. In her heart she knew she had wished to meet him again; to thank him personally for helping her — but to marry him? He was a stranger! Perhaps he would not wish to obey the Major. After all, they were brothers. Her mind pondered over and over again the previous weeks. How simple and predictable her life in the home had been. She had never had any choice, just work and obey. Now the changes were coming so fast and challenging that she had trouble in determining how she felt. Was it fear or excitement — or both?

The journey stretched before her as did the expanse of country. Soon her thoughts turned away from the past and focussed on her present. Seated on the padded leather seat, looking at the little draped window, she was amazed how easy it was to adjust to such a change of lifestyle, when it was a more comfortable one. Would this be what her future in Wales would be like? Why Wales? Nothing seemed to make any sense to her. She reasoned that the Major's brother must be going to run a sheep farm or some such. Perhaps she was to be a farmer's wife, or a landowner's. Whatever the reason, she would demand that she have it fully explained to her before she stepped foot on any ship — and there her thoughts stopped as fear and excitement mingled yet again, because she had never imagined leaving firm ground behind her and being cast off atop a wild and wondrous sea.

9

The coach eventually stopped at a building that looked like a long low cottage. A board swung in the breeze and Tabitha realised that it was a cruck built, single storey inn, covered by an ill kept thatched roof and surrounded by open moorland. The battered old sign swung outside hanging from rusty hooks. An equally worn out painting of a pheasant hanging upside down was painted upon it. It looked ominous in more ways than one, which matched the overall rundown appearance of the place.

The driver came around to Tabitha's side of the carriage and opened the carriage door. He looked sternly at her. Not at all the manner she presumed he would use to address a real 'lady'.

'You get out here . . . miss. I'll light the lamp and try to get a small fire going and you'll wait in there.' He did not pause for her to step out.

'Surely, I'm not going to be left here alone?' Tabitha almost shouted to him as he continued to move away from the vehicle. She felt the cold air on her face and looked around at the dismal place.

'They'll be here soon. I have to return the coach before nightfall. No one else comes this way, lass. It's been derelict for nigh on five years ever since old Ezekiel died of the pox.' His manner was matter of fact, but she could not help but stare at him as if he were afflicted with some madness or other. He honestly expected her to stay on her own in such a place.

'Can't you wait with me . . . just a while? You say they won't be that long. Please stay and keep me company, will you?' she asked him gently, hoping he may take pity on her situation.

'No, miss. That I cannot do. You have been more than aptly provided for. You can stay here on your own. You'll come to no harm.' The corner of his mouth turned up into a grin. 'Soon enough you may be glad of your own solitude, so make the most of it whilst you still can.' He winked at her. The insinuation in his words was deeply offensive to her.

'What's that supposed to mean?' she snapped back at him. Tabitha hadn't meant to but she had not liked his manner at all.

'Time'll show you that. Mind, there's many a lass would trade places with you, so quit moaning and come in out of the cold.' He continued to move towards the old building. She hesitated. He glanced over his shoulder and saw her. 'Please, come with me, miss, and I shall see you settled in and safe before I leave.' He stepped back and did a sweeping gesture with one hand. His intention was clear. She was to leave his carriage, and enter the inn. He had his orders and he was going to see them through. One way or another no doubt he would have his way, or rather the Major would.

Reluctantly, she stepped further into

the cold air and followed closely behind him as he carried her bag over to the door of the inn. He stretched out a hand to turn the iron handle, when he froze mid action. It was as if he sensed something was not quite right. Placing her bag carefully on the flagstone threshold, he raised a hand to her to gesture she should be quiet as he slowly pushed the door open with one finger. Pulling a pistol from his belt he checked its load and then stepped cautiously inside. To his right a door opened into what would have been the main room of the inn with a large stone fireplace and high back chairs at either side. The unswept floor had footprints outlined in its dirt. Tabitha almost squealed at the sudden movement of a mouse as it scurried from one side of the room to the other in the half light. Opposite them in the narrow corridor was another door which appeared to be pushed close.

He gestured for her to stay behind him. The driver was a large man of broad frame. He put his shoulder to it, and with all the might his body and muscle could manage, he heaved against the burden at the other side of the door. It was as if the door had been wedged shut. After a few moments it began to move, giving way to the force he inflicted against it.

Once opened, he stumbled inside nearly falling over the obstruction at the other side. Tabitha followed him inside the room.

'Hell's bells!' he exclaimed loudly.

Tabitha heard the man's shock in his voice.

A man's body lay prone against the door at the other side. Blood stained the flagstone on which he was spread-eagled.

The driver leaned over him and was feeling for his heart's beat. The look of concern on the driver's face told her he knew the man.

'Is he dead?' Tabitha asked, moving around the driver so that she could glimpse the man for herself. A knot formed in her stomach. She looked, yet feared what sight might greet her eyes. What if he were dead? Would he still leave her alone there — with the body? What if they were both found with a dead man at their feet in a derelict inn? She breathed deeply trying to calm herself — as if she was not in enough trouble already. Although she cared for the man's plight, her own was very precarious, and was becoming more involved by the minute. Her own heartbeat quickened.

'No . . . by God he isn't! Mr Simon, you have more lives than a damn cat. If you'll pardon my saying so, sir.' He turned his attention to the man who had begun to groan and move. The driver pulled a silver flask from his pocket and gave Simon some brandy to drink. For a giant of a man he was quite gentle as he tended the Major's brother. It was only then, as the man's face was turned to the dim light from the small window, that she recognised him as her intended husband.

'Simon,' she repeated the name to herself. So that is his name.

'Barratt, you're a sight for tired eyes.' He tried to joke. His gaze found Tabitha's face. 'Ah, but there is a much prettier one, and not covered in dust this time.' He struggled, and tried to sit up. 'We meet, miss, in the most unlikely of circumstances.'

'Where are you hurt?' Barratt asked.

'I took a wound in the upper arm. Whoever shot me knew about the hermitage. I've been running around these woods quicker than a chased hare.' He looked at Tabitha. 'Sorry, miss, about my situation. I am not usually so ill fated.'

'You still live,' Tabitha replied trying to focus on anything positive about their situation. The surprise in his eyes showed as he considered her words and then the smile grew upon his face as he looked back at her.

Simon turned his attention back to Barratt. 'Edgar told me to meet him here, but I took a wound in my arm.

Someone must have mistaken me for a poacher!' He managed to get to his feet. At first he appeared to swoon as if he might faint but then he pulled himself together and although he was unsteady he managed to prop himself against the wall.

Barratt helped him off with his coat. 'Miss, get us a fire going in that small hearth. Use any dry wood and kindling you can find and I'll light it with me flint. I've got to heat the knife and seal this wound before he bleeds to death or catches a poison of the blood.' Barratt fixed a stern look at her as she hesitated for a moment trying to take in what the man was saying. She had tended the sick but no one in the home had ever had a wound like this before.

Simon looked at her. 'Do you wish to wait outside, miss? You look a little pale.'

Barratt stared at her, with more than a hint of annoyance in his voice. 'She'll be no bloody use to us out there, will she?'

Tabitha glared back at the man and noticed that Simon seemed equally annoyed at the man's attitude. She was now fully composed and wanted to help, determinedly so.

'I'll help, Si . . . I mean Mr . . . '

He smiled at her. 'Simon, please. The situation lends itself to informalities. Besides, I'd rather watch you than that ugly brute with a heated blade in his hand.' The smile did not stay on his face for long.

Barratt ignored him and as moments went by and with Tabitha's help the blade was eventually placed in the hungry flames. Tabitha had used the brandy to clean the wound. Barratt examined it and was relieved that the bullet had shot straight through the flesh, but went to great lengths to make sure it was clean all the same. 'Hold his head tightly against your body and do not let him move.'

'Come, man, I'm not a soppy girl!' Simone snapped back angrily.

'No, sir, but you are made of flesh

and blood like the rest of us and, believe me, I'd squeal like a pig if it were me.' Barratt looked to Tabitha and winked at her. She hugged Simon's face to her and he smiled for a moment, a fleeting moment, as the man applied the hot metal against the wound. She buried his face into her bosom to stifle the scream that he was trying to choke back in his throat. Instinctively she ruffled her fingers through his tousled hair as if to calm him, only for a moment until the pain in him subsided. The wound was bound with a strip of cloth that Barratt tore from his own clean shirt. 'I hopes the master will replace this and not deduct it from me pay.'

The words were no sooner out of his mouth than a stern voice replied, 'I may as well, Barratt, as I've paid dearly for every other mistake you bloody fools have made.'

Tabitha stared at the figure in the doorway who had silently appeared. Edgar had arrived. She was still cradling Simon's head in her hands. Edgar looked at her, and she felt ill at ease. She released Simon gently and stepped back.

'Please, don't let me intrude, Tabitha. I'm glad to see that adversity has brought you two so closely together.' He stepped forward and entered the room.

Simon regained his composure as his jacket was eased back on his uninjured arm, placed across his shoulders and allowed to hang loose over his bandaged arm. 'Don't tease Tabitha, Edgar. She is only trying to help me. So tell me, why have you brought her here? This is no place for a young lady to be. I thought you were hiding her at the hall.'

Edgar smiled broadly at him. 'I am glad you value her so. Because, dear brother, she is too much of a risk to my operations. The judge was not at all impressed with the release of a highwayman and his slag, so he created a lot of unpleasantness for those who

103

were at fault. There are many soldiers who would like to hand you two in to gain back their rank, pay or the respect of their man. Besides, Simon, I have the perfect solution.' He paused as he came over and looked at him more closely. 'It appears that your failures have inspired me, because you will now need looking after most carefully as you recoup your health and strength from your ordeal. You will both travel together as your paths seemed destined to entwine. I propose that you will be man and wife and will go to your new home.'

Simon looked at Tabitha. 'What do you mean, Edgar, that we shall travel as man and wife?'

'I meant what I said. You will travel not 'as' man and wife, you will be man and wife.' Edgar's voice was firm.

Simon was watching her, but his expression was difficult to read. 'You know of his plan? Is this agreeable to you?'

'I was never asked, sir. However, it appears I have little choice in the matter.' She tried to keep her anger from her voice as she did not want Simon to think that it was directed towards him. It was Edgar whom she did not like at all. He was arrogant and seemed to enjoy playing at being 'God', dictating their life's path.

'Edgar, you cannot hoodwink or kidnap the woman to suit your own ends,' Simon began to protest. 'This is immoral. I have a right to make my own decisions in life. I am not, and will not be your puppet and, what is more, neither will Tabitha!'

'Neither is true. She is fresh from Miss Grimley's establishment. She is physically strong and attractive. I have this on my cook's best and most trusted word. She can read and write, shows more than average intelligence, an even temper, willingness to work and does not offer her body for favours,' Edgar continued undeterred.

Tabitha glared at him as he dared to smile as he related this piece of information.

'In short, Simon, I have found you a more worthy wife than you could ever have managed to on your own. She even comes with a dowry, a ticket to a new and very different life. What more could you ask for?' He grinned genuinely at the two dumbfounded people staring at him.

'You talk about me as if I was not here. I am a person not an animal or slave.' Tabitha protested, anger rising.

'You are a woman who does not know or appreciate her place!' Edgar's voice was raised higher.

'Edgar, what you do, you do for the best of reasons, I'm sure, but let us take this journey you propose and we shall decide, in our own time, our future, if we have one en route. I can see no reason for forcing our hands.' He sounded tired and Tabitha felt almost as sorry for him and his plight as she did for her own.

'You are going to start your life anew. You, for once, are going to honour your family and start a decent life and future. I have brought a priest here with me, one you are familiar with, Simon, in case you doubt my words. We will, if you can stay conscious long enough, waste no more time and have this matter done with.'

Tabitha was going to protest but Simon placed his hand on her arm. 'It will do neither of us any good. Agree, and then we shall see how our future unfolds.' He was staring at her and she could feel the empathy in his touch.

As he spoke she noticed beads of sweat form upon his forehead. He was trying to be strong, but it was plain that he needed rest and care.

Edgar continued unabated. 'The service and papers will be signed and completed here or I shall leave you both to your own devices. You shall take your chances on your own. Or, do this honourable act and be on your way with my blessing. All the paperwork will be in order. The ship will not wait for you. You must arrive before it sets sail on the high tide.'

'What ship?' Simon asked, obviously taken aback by this latest snippet of information.

'*The Adventurer*, bound for South Wales. Your trunk has been packed and prepared for you, your berth and your necessary papers, land rights and money are all there. I saw to it myself. All you need is your wife and your health for your new life to be complete.' He turned towards the door. 'Father Joseph, may I introduce you to Miss Tabitha Quick and my brother, Simon, whom you know. Now, let the formalities be concluded as soon as possible.'

Tabitha watched the short service unfold before her, as if detached from her body. She heard her mouth say, 'I do'. She saw Simon mouth a similar declaration. He was ill at ease. He shifted from foot to foot, uncomfortable and she sensed also an unwilling player in the fiasco. Her wedding, if she had ever imagined having one, would never have been in such a foul place under duress. Was it even legal — this was not a church, so how could it be? She felt ignorant of the law and trapped. Her senses were alerted when she felt Simon's hand place a band of metal around her finger. The touch of his moist warm lips brushing gently against her own for a fleeting momentary kiss brought a strange sensation to her, unlike the fear she had felt when Edgar had stolen a kiss from her. She didn't know why it should feel so different. His deep brown eyes looked into hers. They were like his brother's but even in the half light she could see clearly that they had more warmth to them.

'There will be plenty of time for you two to become acquainted on the voyage. Interesting place this, once an inn, then this room was used as a chapel, never more a jug of ale to be had here. Shame then the flock fled. Wonder why?' Edgar grinned then, looking pleased with his arrangement, said brusquely, 'Come, we must escort you both forthwith to *The Adventurer*.' Edgar had given yet another order to be obeyed. They were bustled out into the yard where Barratt returned to his coach and left them. Tabitha and Simon were to travel on horseback, with their own guard of men, toward the toward the harbour town.

'Will you be able to ride, Simon?' Edgar asked, almost as an afterthought.

'Yes, you don't need to worry about me, big brother. You have done quite enough of that already.' There was a note of open sarcasm in Simon's voice.

'Good,' replied Edgar. 'For you will have months in which to rest whilst at sea . . . ' he looked back at Tabitha, 'and take great care of him — he is your life now.'

They started riding apace. Her horse's reins were held by Edgar as she had never ridden before and just needed to try to hang on and stay on the animal's back. She had been told to forget modesty and sit astride it. Tabitha thought this was an excellent idea as the animal was so high from the ground. Once she started to move with the horse, her mind was able to think about other things. She wondered how many months it could possibly take to sail to Wales? Then her mind pondered what she should do as they neared the harbour, because she was now Simon's wife and, as such, she was legally his. Was this really her new life? Was it her destiny or God's desired fate for her? Perhaps it was her chance to start life over . . . anew, as Edgar had said. It was then she realised what was happening to them and she nearly screamed with fear and at the stupidity of her own naivety. Yes, they were going to start life anew in South Wales, and Edgar had been toying with her because he was sending them both to . . . New South Wales in the colonies!

10

It was nearly dusk when they finally descended a steep hill from the edge of the moor that led down to the busy harbour town. The salt sea air held a chill as the wind blew in gusts from the rough, as yet unseen, sea. Tabitha could hear waves crashing in the distance and pictured in her mind's eye the rugged cliffs and rocks that were said to feature along this stretch of coast. She had often wished she could see the sea, but never under such circumstances as these. Strange feelings of both excitement and fear filled her, as she had never before visited the coast. However, she had never dreamed or wanted to venture upon it. Birds kwaarked over the roofs of the houses, circling then settling on the higgledy-piggledy edges. New South Wales would be like going to a different world.

Instead of riding down the main street towards the harbour itself, Edgar led the small group into the cobbled yard of a house on the edge of the town. The small space they found themselves in soon filled with the group of horses and riders. Two soldiers stayed by the gate and seemingly kept watch.

No lights were brought out of the building. Instead, a man and a woman appeared through a narrow doorway at the back of the building as they arrived.

They seemed to be wrapped in well worn clothes and were shabby in appearance. The man wore his long hair tied at the nape of his neck. 'Ah, here yer be. We were wonderin' if things had gone wrong, sir,' the man was speaking quietly. He was no more than a dark shadowy figure, a silhouette to Tabitha, in the dim light. His legs in the half breeches looked spindly.

The woman with her cloth cap and shawl flapping in the breeze ran over to Simon who was slumped in the saddle holding his arm to his side. 'Sir, you're near to droppin'. We'll get yer inside an' see yer tended,' she said with an edge of compassion barely detectable through her rough voice. To Tabitha she appeared to be the perfect match for the man, as she was as short and round as he was tall and wiry.

The woman looked around at Tabitha, as if realising she was being watched by her. The moonlight caught the woman's face; it looked hard to Tabitha, wrinkled and quite cynical; a woman used to working in the sea air as if the salt had taken away the very youth from her skin. 'Is this yer maid?' she snapped back at Simon. Her attitude showed only contempt toward Tabitha.

'No, that she is not,' Simon replied and then gingerly slipped off the horse, leaning heavily against the animal. 'This lady . . . ' he glanced at Edgar who raised a quizzical eyebrow at him, then at Tabitha. His expression was difficult to read in the poor light, but his voice declared loudly enough, 'This lady is my wife, madam.'

'Good, I'm glad we have put our introductions behind us. Perhaps now we can conclude our business before the whole garrison of dragoons descends upon this place!' Edgar's voice, also low, still came across crisply in the cold night air. 'Make sure she tends him well, and keep a close watch on her until they are both safely embarked upon their voyage.' He stressed this final point.

'Aye, sir, we will. There'll be no need for you to worry about that, sir.' She glanced up at Tabitha. 'None at all. I'll watch 'em as close as they was me own kin.'

Tabitha felt that same tight knot forming in her stomach that she had when first arrested and locked up by Hester Bramble. She was trapped into a marriage and to a future to which she had neither say nor room to manoeuvre her way out of. Her fate appeared to be sealed, as if she had been judged at the assizes, and they had decided to send her to the colonies. What was she to do but conform? Tabitha looked around at the small group of people as they dismounted. The woman's attention was being taken up on seeing Simon safely inside. Edgar watched Tabitha, though. If she rode away now they would catch her, easily hunting her down. Reluctantly, Tabitha had to acknowledge that for the immediate future she would have to fall in with their plans, but somehow, she promised herself, she would escape from them all and make her own way in the world — somehow!

'Help yer man, lady!' the older woman snapped back at her. Tabitha followed her husband as Simon's stooped figure entered the darkness of the inn's doorway. As she expected, the threshold was far from a welcoming place. The rooms smelled smoky, and the rancour of ale, rather than the welcoming smell of a baker's oven, filled the stale air. Almost immediately they had stepped inside the building they were confronted with a narrow wooden staircase. It was almost vertical and appeared to lead up to a room in the roof space of the building.

'Sir, you has to climb up 'ere. There's a nice bed awaitin' for yer both.' The woman glanced back at Tabitha, who could not help but blush. She paused on the threshold, hesitating, reluctant to be trapped in any more rooms, but Edgar cupped her elbow in his gloved hand and moved her forward.

'Your future awaits you. Do not shrink back from it,' he whispered directly to her ear.

Once they were in the low loft space Simon was led to a bed on which he laid down upon the straw filled mattress beneath the wooden planks that separated the occupier from the open roof thatch and its falling dust or insects. Tabitha glanced around at the cobwebs that spanned from the old beams and the roof's rough straw texture. The old wooden floor had not been swept for some time either. It was far from the homely little room she had loved at the hall.

The man left her and the woman to make Simon as comfortable as was possible. Edgar stepped from the rickety staircase onto the bare uneven floorboards.

'Send for Douglas. He'll see to him. Best get you checked over, no time now for fevers.' The woman nodded, and as quickly as her frame would allow, climbed back down from whence they had just come.

Edgar moved over to the bed, bending low, as the space left little room for his tall frame to stand in its customary upright stance. 'Simon, are you still conscious?' he asked his brother, as Simon had closed his eyes and looked amazingly peaceful.

'Yes, Edgar, I am ... sorry to disappoint you,' he added cynically.

'Don't be pathetic, man! You're scratched, that's all. I would hardly have gone to so much trouble if I wished my own brother ill.' He placed a hand on Simon's forehead. 'Douglas is a ship's surgeon. He will know what is to be done with you. He shall be on *The Adventurer* for the journey, so you will be in good hands,' Edgar glanced over at Tabitha, 'and those of your caring wife, of course.'

'Don't gloat, Edgar. It is not becoming of a gentleman. Why can't I — sorry, we,' he glanced at Tabitha, 'just lay low for a while, and then travel to London?' Simon removed Edgar's hand.

'No!' Edgar raised his voice. 'You have had your chances. The estate will not pay for your careless ways anymore.' Edgar turned to leave.

'You mean you won't.' There was an edge of bitterness in Simon's voice. 'You will follow your folly and risk losing everything. Edgar, you overestimate your own abilities. If I found out about your associations, others will!' He stared at Edgar who glared angrily back at him. It was as if Tabitha had become an invisible witness. She was unsure, however, as to what.

'Precisely, I will not pay one sovereign more to you. Keep your high-handed comments, brother, for your usual companions. I have single-handedly kept the estate alive and our heritage safe. Others are not as foolish as you have been.' He tossed a purse onto the bed beside Simon. 'That is what is left of your share of the fortune. The other papers will be given you in your luggage once you are aboard the ship. Invest it in land and help to build a new nation with your high morals and see if you can achieve at least that.' Edgar waited for a reply. If he was expecting gratitude he was to be disappointed.

'I have been fighting a war, Edgar, whilst you have been playing soldiers here.' Simon had struck a sensitive cord as Edgar almost grimaced.

'You have been playing at soldiers!' Edgar pointed at Tabitha. 'She is healthy and strong, and well capable of giving you sons. You can use the family name, but it is up to you to forge out their inheritance from your own land, far away. Be grateful for my mercy.'

Tabitha felt her temper rise and had to control herself from launching into a tirade at Edgar. However, she knew it would do her no good whatsoever. She could heighten tensions further and that could make her imprisonment more real. So she quietly fumed and listened as Edgar continued.

'Take your own future in your hands and rise to the challenge. Succeed, Simon.' He started back down the stairs, but hesitated momentarily looking back to Tabitha before he was beyond sight down the stairwell. 'Girl, if you run off with that money, I will find you.'

'I'm no thief!' she exclaimed.

'Good, because travelling to New South Wales can be either as a paying passenger or as a convict. You may not enjoy the paying passenger's journey but, girl, you'd know hell on earth if you travelled in chains with the scum below decks. Now obey him, see to his every comfort and earn your own passage.'

Tabitha gave no answer as none was needed or expected. Edgar left them alone. The room was dark, lit only by a flickering oil lamp. Neither spoke, neither seemed to know what to say, as both were lost in their own thoughts and, no doubt, apprehension of what lay ahead.

11

'Miss Tabitha?' He paused momentarily, closing his eyes for a second as if rearranging his own thoughts. 'Mrs Buckley, will you approach so that we may talk to each other honestly.'

Tabitha looked around for someone else then realised that it was her new title.

He propped himself up on one elbow, grimacing as he moved his other arm.

'Don't, please.' She moved over to the bed and sat down on the edge near him, turning to face him. 'Lie back or you shall bleed all over the lovely starched bed linen.' She looked into his eyes as he smiled at her sarcasm. The bed was far from clean and the cloth was hardly fit to be described as linen.

'Tell me, Tabitha, what do you make of our circumstances?' he asked her, his voice sounding both tired and weak.

'I would be interested to know what you think about it, sir. It is you who has, at least in the eyes of the world, the worst of the deal. I had no marital prospects, whereas you have your family's good name.' She was surprised to see him shake his head at her words. She noted the sardonic look in his eyes but continued, 'You appeared to be far from happy with your brother's plans.' She was watching his face for any sign or hint of his true feelings toward her. She needed to know the truth of his abhorrence or concurrence with their situation before she confided her inner thoughts to him.

'It is of no bearing on you or my opinion of you, Tabitha. Your life has been stolen from you, in a sense, your future predetermined by my ambitious brother.' He paused for a moment and looked into her eyes. 'You do realise he brought a real priest with him? We are man and wife, Tabitha.'

Tabitha did realise but she was not going to make comment until she could be sure of him. The marriage was one of ceremony only, at present. They were not yet properly man and wife and Tabitha held to the hope, the only chance she had, that it would not be consummated. 'It is your future also, Mr Buckley. You did not expect to be married to a woman of no rank, money or ambition.'

He grinned, not mockingly but genuinely and she wondered why.

'You have had an education, Tabitha. I believe you are intelligent as well as beautiful, in a homely way. Any man in his right mind would be proud to call you his wife. I do not think that someone of your strength of character can be lacking a modicum of ambition.'

'But you are not pleased,' she challenged him and he averted his eyes.

'I had not decided to marry yet. I have had too many things on my mind, I have issues that need sorting and to put right. Things in which I would not wish to involve an innocent girl; issues concerning my family.'

125

'Woman!' Tabitha corrected, and to herself added 'our' family.

Without humour he looked at her after her sharp reprimand. 'You are quite correct; you are a lady, not a girl. It would be my will to keep you away from here and the trouble that surrounds this place; however, we are both in a prison with no visible chains.'

'Do you plan for us to escape? I shall not be sent to Australia on my own. I have no wish to go at all!' Tabitha had raised her voice slightly as she made the declaration and both looked instantly to the stairs, but there was no sound from below.

'I am in no state to run away, but if, when the surgeon has bandaged me, the opportunity presents itself, would you be willing to make a run for it? Desperate as it may sound, it is what we would have to do.' He took her hand in his. 'I am asking a great deal of you, for my brother is not a man who takes kindly to being disobeyed.'

'Yes, but you must be made strong.

Can you run? You look so weak, Simon.' He moved quickly causing her to stand up nearly knocking her head on the low thatch, when he suddenly sat bolt upright and winked at her.

'You must always deceive your captors. Lull them into a false sense of security.' He held a hand out to her. 'Tabitha, your situation is not of your making. However, if you work with me I shall make things right for you. I give you my word as a gentleman,' he flushed slightly, 'Despite what Edgar would have you believe, I assure you that I am one.'

'How do I know that your words are worth anything? You lie, you act and you are said to be a character who courts danger. Your brother has given every impression that you are constantly getting yourself into situations. So why should I trust you in the least?' She stared at him as he held her gaze. 'You were even acting when you were driving that accursed wagon.'

'Because, Tabitha, you do trust me,

instinctively. You want and need to and you have seen that Edgar is far from an honourable and trustworthy man. Besides, you have no choice really other than to run on your own. You have no knowledge of the streets, nowhere to run and would be found in very little time. Tabitha . . . we need each other.'

He was looking at her, both knowing he had spoken the truth.

'Very well, I accept your offer and protection,' she answered, and was touched when he held her hand gently in his.

Voices were heard from below. Instantly Simon flopped back onto the mattress and closed his eyes, grimacing and gripping the bed cover with his hand as if he was in pain. Tabitha watched his act in awe as she saw the accomplished performance played out before her. She stepped back as the man called Douglas emerged from the narrow stairwell. He 'humphed' with the effort of climbing into the loft space from the stairs.

'Damned hindrance, this place! Could he not have been laid out downstairs?' he grumbled, but carried on stumbling over to the bed. He examined Simon in a very cursory fashion. He swayed, looking unsteady on his feet as if he had been drinking. He poured brandy down his own gullet. A youth had followed him up the stairs. They boy looked at Tabitha nervously.

'Don't just linger staring at the filly, bring me my bag, boy. I need more brandy,' the man bawled.

'I think you've had enough, sir!' Tabitha spoke out when really she had intended not to. Horses' hooves were heard on the cobbles outside. Edgar and his men were leaving. The door below was shut firmly.

'Need anythin', Dougie?' the man shouted up the stairwell.

'No, my good man, I have everything I need here.' He looked at the bottle of brandy and chuckled. I shall see to everything as I always do. You go on. I'll stay with the patient. We'll see them embarked at high tide. You tend to the cargo.'

'Good, sir. Send the lad to the 'Heart and Spile' if yer need anything. Their case is on the gig ready to take down.' The man slammed the door shut and Douglas looked at Tabitha. 'My dear young thing, you should lie down and rest; it'll be a long journey and make no mistake.' He smiled. 'Don't be disappointed, you will have plenty of time for you and your young man to be together en route . . . no, don't blush, ma'am. I am a man of medicine. As I was saying . . . in the months that lie ahead.' He winked at her, as if he understood her thoughts, when he had no idea of the contempt for him that ran through her mind.

'I'm fine, sir. I am extremely patient by nature.' She smiled sweetly at him remembering what Simon had said about misleading one's captor. 'Do you intend to travel with us?' she asked, seeing no sign of movement from Simon. He was either asleep or pretending to be asleep.

'No, lass, just staying long enough to see you two tucked into your little cosy cabin and safe on your way.' He smiled broadly and lay down on the bed next to Simon. The boy sat down by the stairs, watching everything but not saying a word.

She wondered just how much Major Edgar Buckley actually did care about his brother. It did not look as though they could possibly escape. Reluctantly, she sat on a low wooden stool and rested for as long as she could, not able to sleep, nor stay alert as the next hour dragged onwards toward the dawn.

12

At a late hour of the night, what seemed to Tabitha to be approaching the dawn, the sound of someone climbing the stairs stirred her from her sleep. She had forgotten where she had finally laid her head, but discovered it was next to Simon. Resting on the edge of the bed he had placed an arm around her, she had not felt as though it was a possessive gesture, more one of protection, for which she had been grateful, and lying there in his arms she had found some peace.

The flickering light from an oil lamp illuminated the spider's web above them. It swayed, shortening and lengthening the shadows. She'd rather it hadn't, but she sat up and gently nudged Simon, as the man had returned to fetch them. He opened one eye and looked straight at her, then, with the help of her outstretched arm she helped him to sit upright. She was sure he had been awake already and knew he was also able to move a lot easier than he gave the impression to the man. However, if his little subterfuge offered them some sort of advantage she would support it as best she could. Douglas, the ship's surgeon, snoring loudly, still lay flat out on the other half of the bed.

'Come on, you two. It is time to get you on board that ship.' The man kicked Douglas' leg unceremoniously. 'Wake up or you'll miss yer ship, man!' he almost shouted at him.

'What!' Douglas opened his eyes wide and blearily looked around him, obviously disoriented. Where's Toby? Where's the damn boy?' Douglas shouted as he sat up, and then held his head in his hands. 'Damn him, the ungrateful wretch! He's flaming scarpered.' He took his silver flask of brandy out of his pocket and took another swig of it.

The innkeeper looked at Simon. 'Down the stairs, please. Your trunk is on the wagon already. Everythin's taken care of for you.'

Simon stood up, ignoring the remonstrations coming from Douglas. 'It would appear you have thought of everything,' Simon said bitterly as he took Tabitha's hand and led her towards the stairs.

'Just obeying orders, sir. There's nought personal in it, you understand.' He shrugged his shoulders.

'What's done's done. Best be makin' what yer can of it, eh? Don't go makin' more trouble for yourselves.'

Simon did not bother to look at him; he merely replied dolefully, 'Yes, I understand very well, man.' He walked awkwardly, stooping slightly as if still in some pain.

Tabitha looked at Simon; she was apprehensive, not wanting to leave her country, yet desperate to get away from these horrid people. He nodded and pointed to the stairs. She had no reason to, but she could not help it, she trusted him and he had her. Once down in the cold night air they were accompanied by two armed men and a reluctant and grumbling Douglas.

'Quiet, Douglas,' the man said angrily. 'Do yer want to wake the whole neighbourhood up?'

'Well, you don't know how much I paid for that lad. He was goin' to be me own cabin boy. Don't suppose we could go by the orphange and pick up another one?' The man looked as though he was in a state of shock, realising he would have to cope on board ship alone.

His comment was met with open scorn, from all present. Tabitha could not imagine how a child would feel being dragged from their bed and thrown heartlessly on such a voyage. It was hard enough for her, an adult, to come to terms with events, let alone a child.

★ ★ ★

Within the half hour she found herself boarding a ship. A strong wind blew and as she held her bonnet on with one hand she glanced up seeing the ruins of an old abbey upon the headland. She prayed that God had not forgotten her because she had said many prayers since leaving the home, each as sincere and desperate as the last one. It seemed that no sooner had one trial been removed than she was thrown headlong into the next. Simon still held her hand. Her led her toward the steep stairs that led to the middle of the lower deck.

'It is sometimes easier to descend them whilst facing the stairs,' he offered her the advice.

She looked at him. 'Backwards?'

He nodded and showed her how. As he descended he watched her worried face and whispered, 'Tabitha, your future will be happier with me than you imagine. I give you my word.' He winked at her, and then waited for her to climb down. She joined him and saw that at either side of the deck the walls

136

of the ship were lined with very small rooms.

'That's yours.' A sailor pointed to a narrow door to the left of the stairs. He stood on the bottom step looking at them. It was apparent they were to enter it and not be left to escape up onto the main deck again.

Simon opened the narrow door and Tabitha grimaced as she saw a bed at one side of it, barely long enough to take Simon's length, or wide enough, she thought apprehensively, to sleep two people. At the other side was a ledge, which was supposed to be a table. Their trunk was wedged under it and a jug, bowl and bed pot, were placed on the floor in between. She stared at Simon. They were by necessity as close as could be. It felt airless and worse, so temporary a makeshift room that she could tell the wooden walls could be removed as and when required. Nothing solid to give her a sense of security or peace.

He patted her back and asked her to

sit down upon the bed. 'It is not the most luxurious of accommodation, but I can assure you this will be the best the vessel can offer apart from the Captain's own cabin.'

His words did not comfort her. 'How do we escape?' she asked, longing for him to come up with a sensible well thought out plan.

'We don't, Tabitha. Not here, not now. We simply can't.' There was almost a note of apology in his voice.

She stared at him, but he merely shrugged his good shoulder.

'We sail with the tide and wait our turn. If all goes well, we shall be on land again within a couple of days.' Simon placed her hand in his. She felt its warmth. He smiled at her and she stared into his eyes. If only, she thought, they had time to know more of each other first. Perhaps they could indeed find love. She liked him, but their time for that seemed to have been removed with their choice — free will.

She saw a nervous smile cross his

face. Tabitha cleared her thoughts and tried to dismiss such notions. She needed to think clearly.

'Tell me, Simon, what plan you have, for I shall not rest here unless you share the truth with me. I don't like being trapped in confined places.'

'Tabitha, on shore you are an outlaw now. My brother believes he has given you a great chance and myself a companion. Thwart his plans and he would have you clapped in irons and transported if you cross him. I would not be able to help you then.' He heard footsteps on the deck and kissed her tenderly, then whispered, 'My intentions will be revealed, all in good time, Tabitha — all in good time. Please try and find it in your heart to trust me until then at least.'

There was a brief knock on the door — just two taps. Simon stood and opened it to see a figure standing there dressed in sailors' slops. 'This was delivered by a boy for you, sir.' A letter was passed from the sailor to Simon, who gave him a coin in return. The man left quickly and Simon closed the door.

Tabitha watched as he opened the note then placed a corner in the flame from the lamp and carefully watched it burn itself to ashes in the bed pot. 'Tabitha, it is just as well that we are aboard ship. Matters have spiralled out of my hands. We should pray that this ship sails on time. We would be well advised to stay here for now and do not attempt to get to shore. Edgar, it appears, has done me a bigger favour than even I could have imagined. The boy did well last night. Trust me.' She could tell he was in earnest, and she did.

13

Simon stood for a moment leaning against the narrow doorway. The gentle motion of the ship made him adjust his balance. He still held his arm close to his side. Tabitha wondered what the note had said. What did he mean when he said events had moved on?

They had watched a few other passengers arrive and claim their small cabin spaces around the deck. A priest, looking somewhat anxious as he adjusted his eyes to the dim light, nodded at them as he passed by. Another couple nearly fell as they descended the eight or so steep steps. They seemed to be embarrassed by the fact that they fell against each other and were forced into each other's arms. The man helped the young woman stand erect and sniffed the air, walking away with her following crestfallen behind him. Simon smiled and shook his head, glancing down at Tabitha. 'Shall we be so easily embarrassed, wife?' he whispered and winked at her. 'Don't worry, Tabitha. We shall be fine.'

She knew he was teasing her, and she grinned back at him. 'How can we be so withdrawn, husband, when we have shared so much together already in such a short time?'

He smiled warmly at her but then acknowledged the greeting of a man with his family. The wife looked already pale and the children, one of each gender, were excited by their new adventure. Perhaps, she wondered should she abandon her fear and harness some of their youthful spirit — enjoy the adventure fate had put before her? Finally, a single man doffed his hat and nodded to them, followed by his manservant carrying a heavy bag.

Introductions, Tabitha presumed, would come later at dinner. For now everyone seemed to have an exaggerated sense of excitement or dread about them. Tabitha thought it was all pretence, a show of bravado on the men's part, as the ladies in particular showed concern when they saw their new accommodation.

Sailors ran or walked by, too busy to pause or to answer the questions on the lips of the new arrivals. Meanwhile, from above came the ominous sounds of orders being shouted. Chains were clanging, midshipmen shouted orders and foul language was being exchanged by the sailors, followed by more shouts and a cacophony of clanking chains as the human cargo was brought aboard.

Simon looked at her. 'They always take some convicts out on this ship. It is why the fare paid is lower than on the normal supply ships. I think you have heard and seen enough for now.' Carefully he removed his coat. He grimaced as he lifted it over his injured arm.

She stood to help him, hesitating as to whether she should ask him now if he needed her to help. He closed their door behind him. 'I suggest you do the same, Tabitha. It will become very hot in here once everyone is aboard and we make our way across the sea. Besides, there is much that I have to tell you and I think now would be as good a time as any to start to explain something about myself.' They sat side by side on the bed.

'I was hoping you would, Simon.' She soon realised it was no more than a number of planks lashed together and covered by a roll up mattress. Tabitha had lifted the edge and peeped under the mattress as she sat down — fortunately it was freshly made.

'It can easily be removed and dissembled if it needs to be,' he explained, as he smiled at her. 'It is far better than most will have for their comfort — really,' he added as she raised an eyebrow at him.

'I will make this promise to you, Tabitha, that when we make our new home you shall have a fine bed on which to lay your head.' He undid the bow of her bonnet and lifted it from her head. 'That's much better, you are pretty, and have the most beautiful hair. I should like to see it brushed out and free.'

Tabitha looked into his eyes; they seemed to draw her to him. She liked him but she hardly knew him, yet more and more she knew that she wanted to consider him as a true friend. From somewhere deep inside her she found the confidence to ask him the question which was bothering her. His close physical presence made her question more urgent; she had to understand what indeed his intentions toward her were. 'Tell me, Simon, do you really view us as man and wife?'

'I shall be honest with you, Tabitha, I had no intention of taking a wife; certainly not of my brother's choosing or his insistence. Circumstances change, though, and sometimes we find ourselves wrong-footed, or perhaps in our case, right-footed; that we shall have to see.' His smile faded.

His words could not help but

unnerve her. 'I thought we were to escape?' she asked nervously.

'Tabitha, we are escaping.' He gently rubbed her cheek with his finger as if lost in thought, then as her cheek coloured he removed his hand and continued, 'I have been placed in an impossible situation. I returned from the wars, tired, bitter and without a clear view for my future. I wanted to help my country recover from the effect of these perpetual wars and, at the same time, stay away from Edgar. He is so full of his own importance and is determined that the 'heritage' he is so proud of should be protected at all cost, that I sought a more useful path. That is, until I decided what to do with my own life and future.'

He bit his lip, again thinking, she supposed, of how much he should tell her.

'But why did you not seek to stay in the army? Surely that is where you could have helped the most,' she asked innocently.

'Because I had seen too much death and had lost too many friends who thought to be heroes. So, I purchased my way out and returned to England, much to Edgar's disgust. By this time he had formed his own role with the militia and made himself a position of importance in the area. I was, he told me, an embarrassment to him. He considered me to be a coward and, therefore, a failure. Sometimes I thought he would have been happier if in fact I had died out there in a strange foreign land. He might have even had a statue made for the grounds of the hall in my honour.' He chuckled to himself, but it was a laugh with no mirth held within it. I tried to prove myself worthy of the family name which meant so much to my dear father, and enlisted in the service of the country as a Revenue Officer. I did not tell Edgar what I was doing or of my intentions. He would have considered it far below my station in life. I decided I would establish myself first and then when I had discovered something of note, a major smuggling ring, then I would tell him. It was my intention that together we would be able to work side by side to clean up the trade. To this end I rode the length of the coast, often travelling incognito. In the army I was in the Rifles and was used to skirmishes and going behind the enemy lines. It was what I enjoyed doing most. What is more, I discovered a natural ability for it — that is why I still live.'

She was fascinated by his story and realised that, although he had a youthful charm about him, he must be at least five years older than she, perhaps more. He was a man of far greater worldly experience than her which she found attractive in itself.

'After some months I soon uncovered a large well-organised gang. Instead of reporting back to my officer at Whitby I did as I had planned to do and confided my findings to Edgar. I aimed to impress him; however, he called me a bloody fool and said my findings would be his undoing if I spoke to the authorities of them. My dream of us working together to smash them was shattered and I found myself an unwilling participant in their activities for a short and confusing time. You see, I have always respected my elder brother,' he paused and clasped his hands together, 'if not perhaps loved him.'

Tabitha looked at his strong but tired face and realise that this was a man who should be loved, who needed to be respected and, perhaps, could be both by her. She placed her hand on his.

'So what went wrong?' Tabitha asked, wondering how he could have almost been arrested for the very crime he was supposed to be stopping. She saw his knuckles turn white as his fist clenched more tightly under hers.

'I had not realised, never even contemplated for a moment that Edgar was the person controlling the entire contraband ring. He was their banker. So in a way he was quite right, I was stupid.' He shook his head and released his hand from hers, stretching his fingers out.

Tabitha could see the hurt in his eyes. Instinctively, she felt empathy towards him.

He saw the look in her eyes and seemed to sense her compassion and was taking comfort from it. He placed her hand in his once more.

'I should have turned him in.' He looked into her eyes. 'I failed because I could not. He is my own flesh and blood and the disgrace it would have brought upon the family name he, supposedly, cherished, would have destroyed him and possibly me. I had to live with the decision, whichever way I moved. So I was caught in a trap of conscience, tormented at the thought of destroying everything my father had valued.'

'You did what you thought was right, Simon. Would you report him now, if you could?' she asked. 'After all he has done . . .'

'I haven't told you everything, Tabitha. I discovered something far worse. This time I had to act my part well. It was when I was asked to stop by the home, your old home; you see they hid plenty of the goods within its walls and in return received regular 'donations' towards the upkeep of the orphans. I befriended your Miss Grimley. She was at her wits end worrying about some of the girls who had been found employment at the hall. I started to pay more attention to Edgar and his contacts. I am not ashamed to say I spied upon him and his correspondence.'

He was staring at his feet and Tabitha thought that he was not proud of it either. 'You mean that smuggling paid for my upbringing?'

'Partly, yes. However, I discovered something far worse than mere theft from the Crown's coffers. There was a more sinister trade going on than that of brandy, tea and cards, and it was happening under Miss Grimley's nose.

She had smelt something was wrong but she had no proof and no way of knowing just how foul the stench was. Your friends, the girls who left before you never wrote back, did they?'

Tabitha shook her head. 'No, not one of them. Sally, my best friend promised to write, but no letter ever arrived. I thought the home kept their letters from us so that we would not ask too many questions before it was our turn to go into service.'

'They were orphans or discarded children with no one to speak for them. Perfect victims, I suppose.'

Tabitha felt a cold shiver run down her spine as he used the word 'victims'. 'Tabitha, I volunteered to pick you up because I wanted to see if her fears were true. Only things went badly wrong. A passing group of soldiers intervened.' He patted her hand. 'You know what happened then. We jointly became outlaws — my lowest condition to date. When Edgar heard he decided he could rid himself of me for good, legitimately. Fortunately, I had never told him that I was still working for the Revenue service. He had rather conceitedly told me that he was in charge of operations before I had the chance to explain how I came to discover his gang.'

'You mean he still does not know, Simon?' Tabitha saw a broad smile spread across his face and she realised Simon was in fact the smarter of the two brothers. Certainly, he had more honour than Edgar. He was brave.

'I had intended to tell him when I arrived at the inn. However, I was injured, and before I could gather my senses I discovered that, as usual, he had made plans for the pair of us. If I'd spoken out about my work then we would both have been placed in danger. The priest could have been performing our funeral rights, so I decided that under the circumstance presented to me I much preferred the thought of our wedding.'

'So, to answer your question, no, not

before we were placed on this vessel. Tabitha, instead of selling you on through opium dens in London, Edgar had decided you could serve a better purpose by keeping me happy instead. Your face was known. You had become an outlaw and that meant you did have people who, for the wrong reasons, were looking for you. He either had to kill the two of us or remove us from the area. You had become a bigger a risk than me in his eyes because he has always underestimated me.' He paused and stared at her.

'I was destined to be sent to London? To . . .'

'Yes. So you can see that we have been saved from a fate far worse than this.' He glanced back at the bed. 'Marriage is a state to be proud of, Tabitha. I will not force you in any way to . . . to do anything against your will.'

Tabitha blushed and returned to their conversation quickly. 'But, Simon, what about Miss Grimley and the other girls?' Tabitha felt sick as she remembered her friend, Sally, who had naively gone out to her new life with enthusiasm and hope.

'That has been dealt with. I could not stand by and watch innocence be corrupted. He went too far.' Simon shrugged his shoulder.

'The note?' If she was to trust him, he had to show that he too could trust her.

'Yes, the note. It was telling me that the dragoons were on their way to arrest Edgar, and several key members of the gang. I just hope we set a sail before they arrive on shore, for I have no doubt Edgar will try to implicate me. He will not let me escape with these, and you too.' Simon produced some sealed papers from the inside pocket of his coat.

'What are they, Simon?' Tabitha saw that now familiar smile cross his face again.

'Bonds and drafts to be drawn on a London bank. We travel there first before the ship sets sail to Australia.' He kissed her cheek tenderly. 'I have a promise to fulfil to Sarah, Miss Grimley, and then we shall decide upon our future.' He kissed her hand tenderly.

Tabitha was surprised when she felt a stab of jealousy. Was it because Miss Grimley was on first name terms with him and therefore knew him far better than she did? Or was there another reason for her feelings? She had never known what Miss Grimley's Christian name had been and had looked upon her as a surrogate mother — she stared at this fine educated gentleman acknowledging he was her husband.

The ship began to move with a different type of momentum. Simon quickly left the cabin and climbed the stairs to the main deck. Tabitha followed and discovered the ship had in fact set sail. It was leaving the shelter of the harbour and heading for the open rough sea. Tabitha felt a rush of excitement as the cold air bit into her face. She looked at Simon and he, too, was smiling. 'I must make a note that you are not an obedient wife.' He placed his uninjured arm around her shoulders and drew her to him. For that single moment she felt a happiness that had escaped her throughout her life, a feeling of belonging — the start of being loved.

The sight of red jacketed men riding along the quayside caught their attention but it was too late for the ship to be stopped; it had left the harbour and Edgar's figure was soon seen surrounded by the approaching dragoons.

'Now, dear Tabitha, we have a race against time for I need to assure our funds and catch the next ship out of London, as soon as we possibly can.'

'Will we like Australia?' she asked nervously.

'We shall never find out, I sincerely hope, if I have my way, dear Tabitha. For I have no intention of ever going there.' He drew her to him and kissed her tenderly on the lips. The kiss seemed to span moments in time, stirring up strange emotions within her body. She was sad when he broke the moment and took her away from the strong winds to the shelter of the small cabin.

No words were spoken as none were needed, for this was their time to be alone.

14

By the time Tabitha and Simon emerged for dinner with the captain, they had become, in a true sense, man and wife. Tabitha left all doubts behind about how they felt towards each other on shore. She was a woman and he, her husband, was a fine man, by her own standards and choice.

As they dressed for the meal they were quite silent as they learned how to move around each other in the limited space available. Tabitha was filled with so many emotions that she simply did not want to spoil anything by saying the wrong thing. In contrast, Simon appeared to be lost in thought and was dressing almost by habit. Finally, her hair was fixed and as ready as she could make it for what was to be another new experience to her; because although she had been trained as to how to dress a lady properly, she had never perceived a situation arising where it was to be her sitting at such a table or occasion. Simon was watching her as she finished her preparations.

'Tabitha, I had not meant to . . . what I mean is, I had planned to give you more time to decide . . . '

His eloquence had left him. Tabitha saw a vulnerable side to this otherwise daring man.

'I made a decision, Simon.' She smiled at him. 'Ready,' she declared, and placed her gloved hand upon the small latch on the door.

He took her hand in his own. 'Tabitha, I want you to know that I . . . ' he swallowed, and for a moment seemed at a loss for words again. His face had such a serious expression upon it that Tabitha's heart started feeling slightly heavier. What was he thinking? Did he regret their impulsive action? Then an empty feeling overtook her. What if he was disappointed with her in some way. Would he wish to end their relationship in London?

'Tabitha, I . . . '

Simon did not have the chance to finish what he was intending to say because there was a tap on the door. 'The captain requests your presence at his table, sir.'

'Later,' he whispered to her. Simon opened the door and let Tabitha step outside. She smiled at the uniformed man who was tapping on all the cabin doors. Their fellow passengers emerged and were waiting to be escorted to the captain's cabin.

The table was laid out with a fine linen cloth, crystal glasses, porcelain and silverware. Tabitha looked at it in amazement wondering how they could possibly eat at such a fine table whilst the ship was moving with the motion of the sea.

The captain himself was a small man who stood proud in his uniform. 'My fellow travellers . . . ' He welcomed them with a sweeping gesture of his arm. 'Please take your place at my table, for we shall be in each other's company for many months to come.' He stood until all his guests were seated.

Simon had waited for Tabitha to be seated before taking his place next to her. Although he smiled pleasantly at those present and answered questions politely enough, he seemed to be preoccupied with his thoughts.

Tabitha looked around at the mix of faces; some looked decidedly pale. She realized that not all were looking forward to the ordeal. She could not imagine what the conditions below decks were like. As she ate her food she put all such thoughts from her mind. Tabitha had learned of late how to survive in this world; a harsh lesson it had been, but then she looked at Simon and corrected her thoughts — not totally.

'Tell me, sir,' Tabitha listened as Simon addressed the captain, 'when do we put in to London?'

There was a pause in the conversation as the men looked from one to another.

'My dear, Mr Buckley, I am afraid you are misinformed. We do not travel by London.' The captain appeared surprised at Simon's apparent lack of knowledge about such a challenging journey. Tabitha felt for him as his question had made him look somewhat ignorant, or perhaps even irresponsible.

Simon's colour deepened; however, he made a valiant effort to regain his composure and converse throughout the rest of the meal.

The person who spoke the most was the single male who was more than willing to explain to Tabitha that he was keen to draw all the new species of plant, insect and reptiles that he could for his work. He had apparently devoted his life to this aim, gathering as many sketches, samples and notes on the new world as humanly possible. Tabitha wondered how they would survive months of his unabated enthusiasm for his task, or if he were just excited by the onset of the huge undertaking. Time, she thought, would tell. Simon was holding a conversation with other guests so Tabitha engaged this strange young man in her own conversation, listening to him earnestly and taking in the detail of his plans. Simon fidgeted by her side. She could feel the tension rising within him and sensed that he was not pleased with her singular conversation with a young man. However, she was flattered that he watched over her.

They were the first to retire to their cabin. Simon shut the door with more force than he had intended to, causing the flimsy structure to vibrate. He swung around and lifted the lid of the trunk that had been prepared for them. Anxiously, he searched through their belongings.

'Damnation, that man knows no shame!' He closed the lid, turned and stared at a bemused and anxious Tabitha. On seeing the concern upon her face he sighed, 'I'm sorry. I am acting like an ill tempered buffoon, although you appeared to be completely unaware of it as you were so engaged in your conversation.'

She smiled at him. 'I was being polite. What were you going to say to me before we left the cabin?' she asked impishly.

He looked up. 'It was nothing.'

'Please tell me, Simon. If it was worth saying at all, then say it now.' Tabitha looked at him wide-eyed.

He sucked in his cheeks as if deciding whether to or not. 'I was going to tell you that you have made me a happier man than I have been for years.' He blushed slightly, and she felt happiness in all its wonder fill her.

She smiled broadly; all worries and insecurities instantly left her.

He looked at her pointedly. 'However, that's as may be, it will not help our situation, Tabitha. Let me explain to you what our circumstances are, and then you can decide whether my concern is justified.'

'Can I make an educated guess at them?' she asked.

He nodded at her to continue and folded his good arm across his injured one. She had seen his discomfort at the table but he had managed to cover up any hint of an injury.

'Your brother gave you papers of some genuine value to exchange for cash. However, in order to do this you must present them at certain banking establishments in London. Am I correct so far?' Tabitha cupped her hands together on her lap. She had instantly understood the impact of the words that they were not going to London had had upon Simon and why.

He unfolded his arms and nodded once more. 'Exactly, which is why . . . '

She lifted a hand to stop him speaking and continued, 'We are not going to London; therefore, we can not present the documents and access the cash. We are, in effect, paupers at sea.'

Tabitha looked at him, seeing that she had grasped the situation accurately, and smiled.

'I fail to see what you find amusing

about our predicament, Tabitha. Love alone will not sustain us.' He stared at her dolefully.

He had used the word 'love' and she smiled at him. 'Nothing, if we were destined to leave England for good. However, we are not. Whilst I was talking to Mr Jamestone, I discovered that we are to put in to another port to pick up some final supplies. We are to dock at Hull, briefly. There Mr Jamestone will go ashore to make a few final purchases and we shall take on essential food supplies before leaving for the open seas.' Tabitha could not contain her excitement.

'Simon, we have been seen leaving on this ship. No one will expect us to disembark at Hull, as no one is supposed to. However, we will and then we can head straight for London. We can offer Mr Jamestone our cabin for extra space for his purchases in return for our safe journey ashore. I have no doubt he will leap at the chance of it because he has not the space he had been originally promised. Then our lives will be our own. We can live anywhere, so long as it is away from the north. We'll be free, Simon.' She flung her arms around him, filled with genuine hope for the first time since leaving Miss Grimley behind. However, he grimaced as she caught his arm. 'Sorry!' she exclaimed as she sat back down. 'Are you not pleased?'

'Yes, dear Tabitha, but we will still leave England so that we do not have to spend our lives looking over our shoulders all of the time, or be associated with the discredit that will attach itself to my family name.' He cupped her face in his hand. 'You are beautiful as well as clever.'

'But you said you would not go to Australia.' She could not help but look crestfallen.

'We won't. I found my home when I was away in the wars. Somewhere I truly love and promised myself that I would return to when I was ready to raise a family. Now it will be ripe for settling, you'll see and you will love it too.'

'In France!' she exclaimed, appalled at the idea.

'No, my love, in America.'

Tabitha was speechless, and it was Simon's turn to smile knowingly at her. 'My wife, your world has not yet settled down, but you will enjoy every minute of it, I promise.' He kissed her passionately, forcing himself to pull away once more. He stood and opened the door. 'I must make arrangements with Mr Jamestone.' Tabitha could not help but reflect upon the trials she had faced in the last few weeks, and breathed deeply. She wanted to live with Simon, of that she was sure, but first she had to accept her life would never be short of challenges with him by her side. She smiled genuinely, because she knew she was going love nearly every minute of it. She flopped back on the hard and uncomfortable bed and whispered to herself, 'Lord, let the future begin!'